"You're being very strong."

Lexie dropped her head against his chest.

Michael's heartbeat picked up speed and a new tension seemed to run from him to her, heading down her spine to her core. She didn't understand why she suddenly noticed how small she felt standing there beside him. Or why it had just dawned on her that his broad shoulders felt as if they sheltered her from any potential evil.

But those big arms and bigger shoulders were also deviling her with out-of-place sensations. Whatever forces had caused a sudden change in the air began to make her feel itchy...and hot.

Available in June 2008 from Mills & Boon® Intrigue

Shadow Warrior
LINDA CONRAD

MILLS & BOON

Pure reading pleasure

*First published in Great Britain 2008
by Harlequin Mills & Boon Limited,
Eton House, 18-24 Paradise Road, Richmond, Surrey TW9 1SR*

© Linda Lucas Sankpill 2007

ISBN: 978 0 263 85965 2

46-0608

*Harlequin Mills & Boon policy is to use papers that are
natural, renewable and recyclable products and made from
wood grown in sustainable forests. The logging and
manufacturing processes conform to the legal environmental
regulations of the country of origin.*

*Printed and bound in Spain
by Litografía Rosés S.A., Barcelona*

To all lovers, married or single, everywhere –
May you live and love with passion for the rest
of your lives! And to my wonderful husband, the
passion of my life. Thank you, Con, for always
being there with support and love!

LINDA CONRAD

Award-winning author Linda Conrad was first
inspired by her mother, who gave her a deep love
of storytelling. "Mum told me I was the best liar
she ever knew. And that's saying something for
a woman with an Irish storyteller's background,"
Linda says. She has been writing contemporary
romances for Mills & Boon for six years. Besides
telling stories, her passions are her husband
and family, and finding the time to read cosy
mysteries and emotional love stories. Linda
keeps busy and is happy living in the sunshine
near the Florida Keys. Visit Linda's website at
www.lindaconrad.com.

Dear Reader,

Do I have a love story for you! Michael Ayze is an arrogant man. He is the "good" son. But when he's faced with an arranged marriage to his late younger brother's widow, all the old secret longings surface to put a wedge between what he *should* do and what he wants to do.

Cultural differences, Skinwalkers and natural disasters add spice to their story. This is a sensual tale of finding and keeping the right person to love. But I enjoyed throwing a few twists into the mix. I hope you'll love reading Michael and Lexie's slightly scary, very sexy love story!

Here are a few Navajo words to help with your understanding:

Dine	The Navajo – also known as The People
Dinetah	The land between the four sacred mountains where legend says the Dine began (the Four-Corners Big reservation, encompassing parts of Arizona, New Mexico, Colorado and Utah).
anali	grandmother (paternal)
atsili	younger brother
bilagaana	white (as in white man)
chindi	the dark spirits who come with death
hastiin	mister, the title for a respected clan elder
hataalii	medicine man
hogan	the traditional housing of the Navajo, built in an eight-sided design. Now mostly used for religious purposes.
hozho	harmony/balance
jish	a medicine pouch (usually worn on the belt)
ya'at'eeh	hello
Yei	the gods of Navajo myths

Enjoy!

Linda Conrad

Chapter 1

Something was off.

The darkened skies turned to a witches' brew of boiling clouds and fire. Lightning spit, striking a dry desert and leaving black scars of burnt sandstone behind. Torrents of slapping, rushing water, which she knew were a rarity on the Navajo reservation, gushed into parched gullies and flooded sage-clogged ravines.

Alexis Ayze took her foot off the gas pedal and turned to check on Jack, who was buckled into his car seat. Oblivious to his mother's growing fears, the little boy slept soundly, in the deep kind of sleep only a child of four who implicitly trusts his world could manage.

Thank heaven. She had to stay strong for Jack, regardless of how tired and terrified she became.

Lexie wasn't sure why she felt so jumpy and edgy. Well okay, maybe going to meet her in-laws for the first

time was a little nerve-wracking all by itself. But as their
son's widow and the mother of their grandson, she was
positive they would welcome her—even though they
had more or less cut her late husband, Dan, out of their
lives long ago.

In pure desperation, Lexie had written to them and
was relieved when they'd called to insist she and Jack
come to stay. They had been her last hope of escaping
Dan's debts and finding a way to carve out a new life
for herself and her son.

The growing thunderstorm wasn't helping her
current state either, despite her familiarity with harsh
storms. During her marriage to Dan, the two of them
had lived in a lot of areas of the world subject to
storms. Every oil field or potential well site had been
fair game for Dan. The North Sea, the North Slope
fields of Alaska and the Permian Basin in West Texas
were just some of the places with plenty of nasty
weather. She'd lived through them all. But this one
still felt…different.

Another sudden spark of dark fire raced across the
night sky and Lexie felt static electricity run up her arms.
It was so black out here. She wasn't even sure where *here*
was exactly. There weren't any highway signs.

At the crack of thunder, Jack stirred in the backseat,
and she stepped lightly on the brakes again. The rain
was coming down too hard to see more than a few feet
ahead, so she pulled off to the right side of the road and
brought the car to a stop. By the time she turned back
to check on Jack, he had quieted down again.

How did single mothers ever learn to cope with the
concern all by themselves? Since having Jack, she'd

gained a whole new respect for what her father had gone through as a single parent.

Lexie wouldn't give her darling boy up for anything on this earth. In fact, she would gladly die for him. But four years ago, if she had known she'd be raising a child all by herself, she might've thought better about having one.

The constant worry was the hardest part. Damn Daniel Ayze for bringing them all to this point.

She swiped at the few stray tears leaking from her eyes. If only her own father were still alive. He would've taken her and Jack into his home in a heartbeat.

The one person who'd loved her more than life had not lived to meet his grandson. In fact, her father's death eight years ago was what had put in motion a complete change in Lexie's world. One that eventually led her right here—taking her son to Dan's family home on the reservation in Arizona.

And she and Jack were almost there. They couldn't have more than a few miles left to go.

She didn't know much about Dan's family. In fact, the only family member she'd even met was his older brother, Michael, who'd defied the rest of the family and had come to their Las Vegas wedding six years ago.

It was kind of eerie, going to live with people she didn't know. But she had no choice. Lexie had promised herself that she and Jack would only stay with her in-laws until she could get back on her feet and finish paying off Dan's debts. She needed their help taking care of her son while she went to work.

The rain began to let up and she stared out past the windshield wipers at what had suddenly become the darkest, blackest night she'd ever seen. Were they lost?

Driving their old sedan from Louisiana had meant a good three-day drive with all the gasoline and motels and food included. At this point she was running low on cash and worried about Jack getting enough to eat. She could skip meals, but he couldn't.

So she had continued driving after their early dinner instead of stopping for another night at a motel in Gallup. But she'd had no idea how dark it could become in this remote, rural area of the reservation. Or how hard the rain could come down. Or that there would be no highway signs after they left the last major turnoff.

Lexie wasn't even positive they were still on the right road. They hadn't passed another car for the last half hour. She turned on the dashboard lights and studied the map again. Had she made the proper turn back there?

Putting a shaky finger on the road marked Navajo Route 7, she followed it northward from the corner where the huge Ft. Defiance Indian Hospital had been located. What an impressive place that had been, all lit up for the night.

They'd turned at the intersection and were still traveling on the same asphalt road. But where was the gravel lane that was supposed to be her next turn? It had to be right ahead. It just *had* to be.

Turning off the interior light and easing back onto the highway, she blinked away more of the petrified tears welling in her eyes. Something *was* off. She could feel it in her bones. Rather than turning back at this point though, she fought her quaking nerves and gritted her teeth in determination:

In another few minutes, she finally spotted what

must be her turn and swung the wheel to take it. They needed to get out of this storm and find safety right now. So as they crept along a narrow gravel road that showed no sign of life, Lexie prayed she hadn't already made one of the most stupid moves of her entire life.

"What do you mean, you're still expecting them tonight? It's already pitch dark. And the storm…" Michael Ayze tried to keep the annoyance and panic out of his voice as he talked to his mother over the phone. His mother knew little of the secret Skinwalker war raging across *Dinetah*, and it would not be smart to upset her more by mentioning it.

"My daughter-in-law called from Gallup to say they wanted to come ahead tonight," Louise Ayze told her oldest son. "She and my grandson have been on the road for many days already. I wanted to bring them under our roof as soon as possible so I encouraged her to continue driving. But now…"

"It's probably all right, Mother," he told her with a calm lie. "Alexis is not familiar with the roads. She's no doubt just a little turned around in the dark. I'll go down to the turnoff and see if I can spot their car on any of the side roads."

Michael carefully hung up the receiver, hoping not to scare his mother any more than she already was. Navajos on the reservation had an inherent fear of the night—even the ones who did not know of the current war.

But he did know, and the knowledge was nearly paralyzing. Swallowing hard, he grabbed up his rain slicker and keys and dashed out to his pickup.

Up to now, he hadn't let himself consider his sister-in-law's visit. His mother had mentioned that Alexis and his nephew would be coming to stay with the family for a while, but he'd pushed the unwanted knowledge aside.

Ever since the day he'd met Alexis six years ago at her and Daniel's wedding, he had tried hard never to think of his sister-in-law. He wasn't always successful, but most of the time he'd managed to suspend his memories of her soft hazel eyes and the slender curve of her neck under the silky, ash-colored hair.

Anyway, there had been many other things besides Daniel's sexy wife for him to think of recently. Most importantly, the Skinwalker war.

As a member of the Brotherhood, the society of Navajo medicine men who had banded together to fight off the evil ones, Michael's days and nights were consumed with finding ways to overpower and outsmart their enemies. The most difficult and scary fact of their war was that no one knew exactly what the enemy looked like. Or rather, the enemy could look like anyone—or anything.

Skinwalkers were Navajo men who had turned to the dark side and had taken up Navajo witchcraft and shape-shifting. But most of the time they kept to their regular human forms and appeared as ordinary neighbors and family members.

All the better to confuse and terrorize the *Dine,* who refused to talk or think about the unnatural and out-of-balance monsters who walked among them.

It seemed the Brotherhood had been making inroads in the war over the last year, though. Few Navajos had been bothered by witches lately and no one had died or disappeared in months.

But Michael was increasingly uneasy about the unholy quiet in *Dinetah*. He'd taken a leave of absence from his day job as a professor of anthropology and comparative religion at the *Dine* College three months ago to search for the ultimate answer to putting an end to their terror.

The Brotherhood had learned that a special map, an ancient guide to long-lost parchments, was missing. The parchments were thought to contain chants and potions which would either kill off the Skinwalker witches—or allow them to live forever.

The map in question had been hidden a year ago by a Skinwalker lieutenant in some kind of double cross of his superior, the Navajo Wolf. But that foolish Skinwalker lieutenant had died before revealing where he had buried the map. Now, both the Wolf and the Brotherhood were racing to uncover the map first.

Their searches had been keeping Skinwalkers and the Brotherhood from skirmishing with each other. But Michael knew it was only a matter of time before the uneasy peace would be over.

He braked, looking up through the windshield as the downpour continued and a layer of clouds descended from the mountain tops. Fog had moved into low spots and wetness dripped from every branch and rock. Rivulets of running water trickled over roadside gravel with a force Michael would not have recognized from the rare rain on the reservation.

Fighting off a shiver, he wondered if this unusually strong storm might be nature's signal that their inadvertent truce with the deadly enemy had already been broken.

Where the heck were his dead brother's wife and child? This was no night for strangers to be out after dark.

Lexie knew she was lost. What she didn't know was how to turn around and go back.

She'd been so positive she'd made the right turn off the asphalt highway back there. But after a mile or two of driving, the gravel road had almost disappeared. Until, finally and miserably, she found herself heading down a narrow, one-lane path with tall brush growing higher than the car on both sides.

How on earth was she going to get out of here? She blinked back another frisson of panic and reminded herself that even narrow gravel roads went *somewhere*. Eventually she would come to a house or another turnoff. All she needed was enough space to turn the car around.

If only the weather had been a little better tonight. True, the downpour had slowed to a drizzle, but misty fog had begun to fill up all the dips in the road. The gravel lane she'd been driving had dips, potholes and gullies in abundance, too.

As if to prove her point, the car's headlights shined on the edge of a huge, dark dip in the road. No choice now but to slow down and carefully navigate the upcoming hill like she'd already done for the last few.

But as the car slowly moved over the edge, she saw that this particular gully seemed a lot steeper than any before. On the way down, her headlights beamed against a puddle at the bottom. She'd already driven through a lot of wet spots on the roads, but it was hard to judge the width of any puddle in the extreme darkness of the cloudy night.

Slowing to a stop as her car came to the edge of the water, Lexie tried to peer across but couldn't see to the uphill side of the gully because of the fog. She put her foot on the brake, closed her eyes and rested her forehead on the steering wheel.

What could she do to keep herself from becoming totally spooked? She had to remain calm for Jack, so she tried a series of small stretches. Would her car be able to get up enough speed in order to climb the other side?

Please let this old sedan make it as far as her in-laws' house. She'd never been very religious and hadn't prayed in years. But this was the time for it.

"You've made a bad mistake. Get out of here."

Dan? The voice seemed to be her dead husband's. Impossible. She must be hallucinating.

She opened her eyes and turned to the familiar voice coming from the passenger seat. There, casually slumped in the seat and grinning the same old non-chalant smile she'd once fallen in love with, was her husband, Dan.

Oh. My. God. Lexie blinked, then swiped at her tired eyes. She bit back a scream and took shallow breaths, trying desperately not to freak out. This was one more time where she needed to stay strong for Jack.

Seeing dead people wasn't a totally foreign concept. Lexie's talent for such things had been immature while her mother had been alive, but definitely there, whether she'd wanted it or not.

Lexie had put that part of her life away in a secret compartment of her mind after her mother's death. Mother had been the one who'd seen ghosts.

Until now.

Why was Dan's ghost here? Why now?

"Am I dreaming?" she managed to say as she tried to stem the shakes. "Or dead, maybe?"

"Neither one," the spirit of Dan's body said. "It's me, and you are definitely not dead. Not yet anyway."

She shot a quick glance at Jack in the backseat, trying to assure herself he was okay. Her child kept on sleeping and seemed fine. Turning back, she frowned at the vision of his father.

"What's going on?" she demanded, as if the apparition were her real husband. "Why are you here?"

He laughed in the same overly charming manner that had once enthralled her but eventually had grated on her nerves. "I'm whatever you want me to be, and I'm here to warn you away."

"Warn me away from what? Will you please stop speaking in code? Would it kill you to say what you mean?"

Her words brought out another bark of laughter from Dan's ghost, and she gritted her teeth to keep from yelling at him. Death did not seem to make her husband any more endearing than he'd ever been.

"I'd say there isn't much that can kill me these days, darlin'."

"R-right." She swallowed hard. "Then at least tell me straight out what you came to say."

The vision of her husband sat up and lightly touched her face. "I've missed you, Lex. That's one thing I wanted to say."

Lexie wondered if she shouldn't be more afraid of seeing a ghost. But she wasn't.

Lexie wasn't scared of Dan's spirit in the least. Instead, she found herself becoming more and more furious at his memory.

Rearing away from his touch, she scowled. "You shouldn't have left us to run off to Iraq. What was so wrong with making enough money at home to pay off your debts? You shouldn't have done anything so dangerous. You had a child to think of."

He chuckled. "Why should *I* have thought of him? You were doing enough of it for both of us." Straightening and shaking his head, Dan continued, "Speaking of dangerous, you shouldn't have come here, Lex. You're in the wrong place."

"I know we're on the wrong road, dammit. Tell me something I don't know. Like how to get out of here."

"You should not have come to *Dinetah* at all. There's great evil on the reservation. Go home."

Evil? "We don't have a home to go to anymore. Thanks to you. And what do you mean by—"

Her words were stopped by a sudden rumble of thunder coming from her left. She turned to look for the lightning flash, trying to judge how far away the bolt had hit. It had sounded close.

She felt the ground move before she fully realized how much trouble they were in. A massive wall of water appeared out of the darkness and quickly covered the hood of her car before she could even catch her breath.

Uh-oh.

She didn't have a moment to think. The sound hadn't been thunder at all, but the roar of rushing water coming straight at them. Where was the water coming from?

"Dan, help us." She turned back, but the vision of him was gone.

Water began seeping around the door into the passenger compartment. She had to get out of here. *She had to get her baby out of here.*

Flipping open her seat belt, she gripped the door handle and tugged. The door wouldn't budge.

She reached for the electric window buttons and discovered the car had died. Without power, none of the windows would open.

Dear God. No!

The force of the rushing water began to rock the whole car. Icy cold water was already covering her feet.

"*Jack!* Wake up, baby. We have to get out of the car." She fought her way to her knees and prepared to crawl over the seat to get to Jack.

Lexie threw herself forward, landing in a heap on the floor of the backseat. Her whole body was soaked through from dropping into the quickly rising water. Shivering, she reached for her child.

"Mommy?"

"Jack. Help Mommy get you out of the seat belt, honey." It took everything she had to keep her voice calm.

"Out?"

"Yes, out—now."

Instead of helping him undo the belt, she trusted him to do it. Grabbing the door handle next to him, Lexie shoved hard. She had to find a way out of the car. The water was already creeping up to the edge of the seat and she could feel the whole vehicle being shoved sideways by the sheer force of the water's current.

The back door next to Jack's seat was locked tight

and refused to budge. Trust the childproof safety windows and door locks to work when you didn't want them to.

"Are you free?" she asked Jack as she reached for him.

"I'm scared." He scooted toward her.

"Don't be afraid. We're going to be okay." She hugged him close and tried to think. "This is a new game, honey. First move is getting into the front seat. Can you do it?"

"Yes," he said and scrambled up and over. "Do I win?"

"Not yet, baby." Lexie wished she was as limber as her child. "My turn."

Putting aside the overwhelming panic, she grabbed the seat and somersaulted over it, landing next to Jack. "You okay?"

He mumbled an answer and she could tell he was beginning to shake. "Move away from the door, honey. I'm going to push it open so we can get out."

Jack inched toward the steering wheel on the driver's side of the car, out of her way. Lexie grabbed the passenger door handle and shoved hard. Miraculously, it opened. Slightly. But when she kept on pushing, the door refused to go any farther than an inch or two.

What were they going to do?

Lexie felt around in the water on the floor, hoping to find something heavy enough to break the window. Of course, there was nothing like that.

She took off her shoe and began to bang it against the glass. Nothing happened except dull thuds.

They couldn't get out and were going to drown. Her baby was going to die. The dark purple fog of hysteria clutched at her throat.

Starting to cry, Lexie beat against the window with her fists. Then she turned, opened the glove box and dragged out everything it contained. Maps. Gas receipts. Cheap sunglasses. But nothing that could break glass.

Jack caught her panic and started to scream. The water covered the bottom of the seat now and gushed through the car, shoving everything toward her and pinning her to the partially open door.

Her little boy grabbed hold of her neck with a death grip. "Out. Mommy, I want out."

She couldn't get herself together enough to calm her child. They were going to die. Hugging him to her, she was lost in great gulping spasms.

All of a sudden, Jack reared back and pointed to the door. "Daddy! Daddy, I want out now. I don't like this game."

Lexie turned in the direction he was pointing just in time to see the already partially opened door wrenched wider. A dark shadow of a man bent down and pulled both her and Jack out of the car and into his arms.

Chapter 2

Dan? Was it really her dead husband's spirit come back to save them?

Everything was cold and dark and wet. But her body was suddenly being hugged tightly against a broad, warm chest as she and Jack were whisked upward. Away from the car. Out of the water and hopefully to safety.

The roar of the water rang in her ears. The darkness made everything surreal. She heard Jack's squeals of terror as she gathered him close and hung on.

Lexie, on the other hand, was quietly holding her breath. Were they going to die? Was that why she had suddenly started seeing ghosts as her mother had before she'd taken her own life?

This whole thing was one terrible nightmare.

By the time Lexie took a breath, Jack had calmed

down and her feet were touching solid ground. And it was abundantly clear, even in the blackness of the night, that their dark rescuer was not Dan's ghost.

Whoever the man was, he was taller, broader, just all around bigger than her dead husband. His warm, solid chest did a lot more than merely hint at him being a living, breathing adult male.

The man made sure she was steady on her feet, then he lifted Jack out of her arms. "My truck is right up the road. Let's get you two someplace warm and dry."

"Uh…wait a second." Lexie didn't want to offend someone who had just saved her life. But who the heck was this guy? Did she dare trust her child and herself with a stranger? A very big, burly stranger.

"That was fun, Daddy. Let's do it again!" Jack didn't seem to share any of her qualms. But then, he thought this man was his father.

The tall stranger had on a yellow rain slicker with a baseball cap pulled down over his forehead, keeping the still drizzling rain out of his eyes. The cap cast a shadow over his face, giving Lexie weird shivers down the back of the neck.

Without waiting for her to utter another word, the man hefted Jack higher against his chest, took her by the elbow and began heading up the hill. At this point, she didn't much feel like dragging her feet—her bare feet. Getting dry and warm sounded too good. But she sure as hell intended to get some answers before she got into a truck with a complete stranger, no matter what Jack thought about him.

Before she could orient herself to the pitch-black surroundings, she was standing next to an oversized pickup truck with one of those huge double cabs. The stranger leaned her against the bumper and let go, but kept Jack in his arms.

"Stay here a second," the man growled. "I've got blankets in the back."

She heard him opening doors and at the same time heard him mumbling something to Jack. In a few minutes, the guy was back beside her, placing a blanket around her shoulders.

"Get in," he demanded.

"But…"

Without warning, he lifted her off her feet with one big arm and slid her into the back passenger seat. "You and your son must sit in the back. It's too dangerous for him to ride in front."

"Wait just a sec…"

The man placed Jack next to her, then reached around her and buckled them both in. His body came within inches of her face. She caught a whiff of his scent and her body had an odd reaction. The deep woodsy smell seemed both thrilling and familiar to her somehow. Maybe the sudden jolt of recognition had more to do with an indefinable, underlying scent of masculinity. Was it simply a reminder of the way Dan had smelled that was catching her imagination? No, she couldn't put the stranger's scent together with Dan's memory at all.

Whatever the reason for it, a bolt of electric impulses tingled through her skin, prickling and stinging along her nerve endings. She couldn't quite understand what was happening to her, and she was still too scared to make sense of the strangely erotic feelings.

She pulled Jack close to her side and hung on for dear

life as the man slammed her door and moved around the front of the truck.

"Mommy." Jack turned his face to look up at her.

"Yes, sweetie?" Out of the corner of her eye, she watched as the stranger climbed into the driver's seat and started the engine.

"The man says he's not my daddy, but he looks like Daddy's picture in your wallet."

"No, Jack. The man is not your father. We don't know him." The engine came to life with a rumble so loud Lexie was sure the man in the front couldn't overhear their conversation. She wished he would explain himself to her as he apparently had to her son.

"Yes, we do," Jack disagreed with a grin. "He says he's my daddy's brother and I should call him *uncle*. What's a uncle?"

"Uncle?" Lexie raised her voice, hoping to be heard by the silent man behind the steering wheel. "Excuse me. Are you my husband's brother—Michael Ayze?"

He gave her a sharp nod of his chin but never turned his eyes away from the windshield. "My mother was worried because you two were late and sent me out to find you," he said over his shoulder. "I guess she had good reason to worry. What were you thinking, driving out on the reservation in the middle of the night?"

Her anger came up fast and strong and completely unwarranted. After all, the man had just saved their lives. Still, what right had he to question her actions? He was only her brother-in-law, not her husband or father—or keeper. She had no intention of explaining about running low on money to such an arrogant male.

Lexie bit her tongue to keep from telling him off.

Silently counting to ten and breathing deeply, she fought to find the right words to keep from alienating her husband's family right off the bat.

She couldn't find any. Still seething, she decided to keep her mouth shut and treat his last comment as it deserved to be treated. With silence.

Happy about the strained quiet coming from his sister-in-law's quarter, Michael knew he should never have said anything to her that was so negative and definitive. At least, not without being prepared to explain why it was wrong to drive alone on the reservation after dark. But he had no intention of trying to tell this Anglo woman about the Navajo Skinwalkers. She wouldn't believe him anyway. Much better they both keep their words to themselves.

His thoughts, however, now those were another story entirely. He couldn't get the fanciful image of being her savior out of his mind. He'd saved their lives and had been her knight in shining armor, her defender against the dark forces.

But hell. That wasn't something a college professor ought to be thinking. Maybe he'd better get his suddenly weird imagination under better control.

The cause of their danger tonight probably hadn't come from Skinwalker evil. Death by drowning would've come simply from Alexis's ignorance of the area. There were many different kinds of dangers on the lands between the four sacred mountains.

The unwanted thoughts of dangerous things reminded him of how his pulse had quickened when he'd gotten his first good look at his dead brother's wife. He'd felt the same erotic rush the last time he'd seen her, six years earlier on his brother's wedding day. He'd been trying to forget it ever since.

He'd defied his parents' wishes then and had gone to the wedding to talk to Daniel. To try again to make him reconsider coming back to the reservation with his new wife. But Daniel had been more determined and independent than ever and had flat out refused.

So Michael had met the bride and stayed only long enough for the wedding. *Elegant* wouldn't have been too strong a word to describe his initial impression of Alexis back then. She'd been dressed plainly for a bride, in a sophisticated ivory sheath. But her sweep of ash-blond shoulder length hair had been all the embellishment the outfit needed. That and those intelligent hazel eyes. The eyes that had drawn him in and made him forget why he'd gone in the first place.

His original assessment then had been that she was much too good for the likes of his half-assed brother, Daniel. Tonight, even soaking wet with her hair pulled tight and dripping, she still looked somehow ethereal and out of place here in rural *Dinetah*. He couldn't get the idea of her being a queenly damsel in distress out of his mind.

Deliberately shifting his focus over to his nephew, Michael shot a look at the kid in the rearview mirror. Going by appearances alone, it seemed clear enough Jack Ayze was a Navajo child. The boy didn't look much like Daniel had at his age, but his golden-brown eyes and angular jaw were definitely attributes of their Big Medicine Clan's roots.

The boy belonged with his family and his heritage. He deserved to be raised in the *Dine* tradition.

All those superfluous thoughts would have to wait for now, though. Alexis and Jack needed to be safe inside his family's home for the night.

For the time being, keeping the two innocents alive and well was all that really mattered.

Not wanting to dwell on seeing Dan's ghost or on the terror of almost drowning, Lexie kept her thoughts tuned in to their rescue. After they settled in the pickup truck, Michael drove them back to the highway and about fifteen minutes farther up the side of the mountain before turning again. It was nearly impossible for her to see where they were going, but she got the distinct impression of heading up a long dirt road.

The complete darkness of the place felt creepy. Lexie had never experienced this much isolation.

Then the pickup drove out of the black night and into a lighted gravel area. Once they had pulled up and stopped in front of a modern house with several out-buildings, she finally began to relax.

Belatedly, it occurred to her she'd never given much thought to what kind of housing Dan's parents would have. She'd been so anxious to get a roof over her child's head, she hadn't considered what that roof might look like. That kind of oversight in planning would have to stop. What if Dan's family had lived in a shack?

A widow and single mother at twenty-eight, Lexie decided it was past time for her to become a responsible adult. From now on, she would plan every move out much more carefully.

As she unfastened her and Jack's seat belts, she saw a short, dark woman come out of the house, stand on the porch and wave excitedly at them. Lexie wanted to go slow with Dan's family until she could formulate some kind of plan for how to deal with having new relatives she didn't know.

But those good intentions disappeared the instant Louise Ayze wrapped her arms around her and hugged her close. "I am so glad to finally meet you, Daughter. Come inside your new home."

Michael swung Jack up into his arms and the two of them disappeared through the front door ahead of her. *Home?* Had Dan's mother said what she thought she'd said?

"Please call me Mother, my daughter," Louise whispered formally as she slid her arm around Lexie's waist and led her all the way inside.

"Oh. Well…" Lexie didn't know what to say. She didn't even know what she was feeling.

Despite her mother-in-laws' rather formal and stilted language, she seemed sincerely happy to have her and Jack here. But could Lexie learn to call someone *mother* again at this late stage? Her own mother had taken a coward's way out, and Lexie didn't want any reminders of her.

The minute she crossed the threshold, though, Lexie realized she'd have no trouble at all calling this place home. Everything about the front room of the Ayzes' home was warm and inviting. A huge fireplace blazed with a crackling, friendly sounding fire. Gorgeous native-designed rugs partially covered gleaming wood-planked floors. Sofas with cozy pillows looked so compelling she imagined herself snuggling into one for the entire night.

Louise, a tiny woman with a straight back and a look of steely determination in her eyes, dragged Lexie through the front room and didn't let her stop to enjoy the homey atmosphere.

"Are you hungry?" Louise asked as they entered a big open kitchen and family room.

"No, but thanks."

Jack must have thought he could use something more to eat, however, because he'd climbed into a big chair and was sitting at the table. Beside him sat two giants, both of whom were hovering over him and talking in quiet tones.

One of the giants was Michael, Jack's uncle, who had saved them. The other man looked just like both Jack and Michael, except for the gray hair at his temples. When Lexie walked closer, all three males turned their faces to look up at her.

Michael introduced his father saying, "Alexis, this is my father, Charles Ayze."

The older man nodded. "Welcome, Daughter."

"Hi, Mommy," Jack broke in. "Grandfather said I could have a cookie. Okay?"

Three sets of warm chocolate eyes watched her closely, waiting for an answer. Three sets of eyes all from the same mold, and all set above the same square jaw and same Roman nose.

Except for having shared similar thick ebony hair and copper-colored skin, her baby's features were subtly different from his father's, especially around the eyes. But Jack looked so like his uncle and grandfather it took her aback for a second. She wasn't sure how she felt about it.

"You may have *a* cookie, sweetheart. But then we have to get you out of those clothes and into bed."

"But I'm not wet anymore and I don't want to go to bed yet."

"Wet?" Louise turned and let her sharp eyes make a head to toe inspection of Lexie, then she swung back around to address her oldest son. "Why did this daughter and her son become wet? And for that matter, where is her car? What don't I know?"

Michael stood to face his mother's inquisition, and Lexie got a good look in the light at the man who had saved her life. She'd known he was taller than his brother, and she vaguely remembered from her wedding day that he'd been broad-shouldered and burly.

His eyes were the one thing she'd remembered the most, though. Those steely eyes, watching her with a thoughtful intelligence, had stuck with her over the years.

Now those eyes were crinkled with fatigue. And his rugged features, contorted in a portrayal of wary innocence for his mother, were still causing a strange reaction in Lexie's gut.

When she'd been a young twenty-two-year-old, she'd fallen for Dan's beautiful, grinning face. But looking at her late husband had never started the same crazy kind of internal sensations that looking at his brother was causing. Michael's quiet appearance was making her knees weak and her whole body tingle. But maybe it was only the lingering effects of her and Jack's brush with death. Lexie fervently hoped so. This sudden sensual pull coming from her brother-in-law could *not* be a good thing.

Michael explained away the flash flood to his mother in lightweight terms. No big deal. They'd go out in the morning and work on saving the car and their luggage. All would soon be back in balance, he told an agitated Louise.

The whirlwind who had asked to be called *mother* suddenly turned into a drill sergeant, issuing orders to all of them. Lexie and Jack soon were plied with hot chocolate and cookies, hustled into hot baths and dressed in borrowed pajamas from storage to wear to bed. Michael and his father were put to work on the phone, making arrangements for the morning.

Lexie was amused and confused by her mother-in-law's fierce control. But she also felt completely safe here because of it. After she put Jack down and then snuggled into her own bed with crisp clean sheets, she surprised herself by falling into a deep, dreamless sleep.

Awakening the next morning to a shaft of growing daylight shining through the window, she found her first thought was of her rumbling stomach. She slid out of bed, pulled on a borrowed robe and went off in search of Jack—and breakfast.

"Are you sure Jack won't be any trouble for your husband?" Lexie asked her mother-in-law as they came back into the house from the barn hours after breakfast.

"Trouble? No child with such an open, inquisitive mind could be considered trouble." Louise smiled and went to wash her hands at the kitchen sink. "Would you like a cup of tea? I have a few minutes before I have to dress and leave for my luncheon."

Lexie had reluctantly left Jack out in the barnyard with his grandfather, who was feeding the animals. She'd been concerned about being separated from her baby in such a strange and different world. But Jack had been fascinated with the sheep and the family's one horse—and with his grandfather, who never stopped talking to him about what being Navajo meant.

She'd finally come to the decision that she trusted her newly found in-laws with Jack's welfare. Eventually she would have to leave him so she could go to work. After all, that was the main reason she'd brought them all this way.

"Yes, tea would be nice, thanks." Lexie washed her hands and then sat down at the table. "Is your lunch today with friends? Or is it business?"

Oops, the question seemed too personal for someone she had just met. But Lexie already felt comfortable around the woman who still insisted she call her *mother.*

Louise just smiled. "My youngest son may have told you that my husband and I are both attorneys, though my husband recently retired in order to have time for politics. He's currently the elected councilman to the Navajo Nation Tribal Council from our local Red Lake chapter."

After putting a teakettle on the stove, Louise reached into a cabinet for cups and saucers. "My own legal work has always been more service oriented. For many years I chose to work for the Tribal Legal Aid office. Now I devote most of my time to various charities. Today's luncheon is a fund-raiser for the Window Rock Navajo EARTH group."

"Earth?"

"Education and Research Towards Health," Louise told her as she poured the tea and sat down. "They do good work for the People. And there is so much to be done."

Lexie smiled as she sipped her tea. It was herbal tea of some sort. Mild and fragrant. Good.

She began to feel slightly inadequate in the company of such a highly intelligent, professional woman. Though Lexie had finished three years of college, when she'd gotten married, she had been working for a casino as a high roller's cocktail waitress. Which had actually suited Dan just fine because he'd always wanted to be a high roller.

During their courtship, he'd told her he came from a family who all had advanced degrees. But since the family hadn't been terribly happy with Dan at the time, she'd never met any of them but Michael. And she certainly had never imagined them to be so refined and intelligent.

Her smile slipped a little.

"Perhaps after you settle in, you'd like to go with me to one of the charitable functions. A new volunteer is always welcome."

The explanation for not going would be difficult to say. Better get it over with. "Uh. I'm afraid it's urgent that I find something to do to earn a living first."

Thank goodness it was just the two of them here talking instead of having to embarrass herself in front of the entire family.

Louise raised her eyebrows. "You and my grandson need money? My youngest son did not provide for his family after his death?"

Lexie shook her head but felt herself blanch. Damn that Daniel Ayze. She hoped his spirit was still around nearby to share in the shame.

If Dan had been alive, she'd be willing to kill him all over again for putting her in this position. With her bare hands.

Without having an easy way to make herself disappear, Lexie shrugged and tried a weak smile. Oh hell. She'd do whatever it took for Jack's sake.

"Do you know much about *Dine* tradition, my daughter? Did my youngest son ever instruct you in the Way?" Louise asked softly without making mention of money.

Lexie shook her head. "Not really. Dan never talked much about his family or his heritage." She thought her mother-in-law's change in the conversation rather abrupt, but anything would be better than continued discussion of her embarrassing lack of funds.

"You have brought my grandson to his traditional home. Does this mean you wish for him to learn about his heritage?"

"Well…" It wasn't why she'd come here, but the idea sounded good now she'd thought of it. "Of course I do. He should be aware of his roots and family."

Louise nodded thoughtfully. "It would be smart then for you to learn to follow the Navajo Way, as well. You could reinforce your child's lessons. Are you willing?"

"I…"

"What are you trying to convince her of, Mother?" Michael Ayze interrupted his mother's thought as he stepped into the kitchen from the front room.

"Ah, my son. You are here just in time. This conversation concerns you, as well."

Lexie's curiosity was piqued—along with her nerve endings. Michael's presence tended to make her jittery, so she wasn't surprised by the heat he'd generated when he walked into the room. But she really hoped he could help translate his mother's true intentions, because

Lexie was becoming increasingly lost by Louise's half-finished ideas and formal speech.

Michael raised his eyebrows, also questioning his mother's meaning. "All right, Mother. Spill it. What's that devious little mind of yours up to now?"

Louise's smile turned to a wry frown. "You know I don't have a devious bone in my body. Such a thing would be out of balance and the antithesis of everything we believe."

Michael's narrowed gaze said he wasn't convinced.

But Louise didn't pay any attention to her eldest son's expression as she turned back around to Lexie. "There are many legends and traditions for you to learn, daughter. My grandson will have no trouble picking up the lessons as a child. The young are receptive to new ideas. Adults find the learning much more difficult.

"So I will expect your brother-in-law to become your teacher," Louise continued. "In the same manner as he does in both his occupations."

"Both?" Lexie wasn't sure what Louise was talking about. She turned a questioning look to Michael.

"You know I'm a college professor," he confirmed without taking his sharp gaze from Louise's face. "But my mother is referring to the fact I'm also a traditional *Dine* medicine man. Part of the calling is to pass on the traditions and oral lessons."

Michael was ready to kill his mother, but he knew she meant well. All of his immediate family was in a constant battle with themselves to find a happy melding of their old traditions and the modern world.

"I see," Lexie said. "But I'm sure you're too busy to

worry about teaching a complete stranger your ways. Are there books I can read instead?"

"Not really. But…"

"Books aren't necessary." Louise interrupted. "You will have plenty of time together to absorb the lessons."

Louise turned and took Lexie's hands in her own. "The basic premise of the Navajo Way is to remain in harmony. Finding balance in all things is what makes you *Dine*.

"And the first lesson in harmony our original mother, Changing Woman, taught us was that male and female need each other for balance. One sex is not complete alone. To stay in keeping with our traditional Way, when one *Dine* spouse dies, another family member steps in and marries the survivor. It maintains the clans and brings harmony."

"What?" Both Lexie and Michael jumped as each exclaimed the same thing at the same time.

For an instant they stared, unbelieving, at Louise. Then they threw sideways glances at each other before both took a step back, putting more distance between them.

Louise ignored Lexie for the moment as she turned to Michael. "Your brother died, leaving a widow and son. You know the traditions better even than I do. Is there any question of you following the Way, *hataalii?*"

Michael knew his mother was using the respectful Navajo word for *medicine man* to remind him of his duty to go along with tradition. But this was the twenty-first century, and the widow in question wasn't even *Dineh*. She would never accept the idea, even if he could.

"Uh." He couldn't get his tongue to work for a second. "If Alexis needs money, I can give her a job or a loan—or both. Until she gets on her feet. But she's an Anglo. You can't expect her to give up her own heritage and abide by an ancient *Dine* tradition just like that."

"Not just like *that*," Louise said with a scowl. "Take some time together. Teach her the Way. She's already said she wishes to help her son by learning." Louise smiled brightly. "Thirty days ought to be adequate. I'll use the time to plan a wedding."

Chapter 3

"You're sure this wasn't a Skinwalker attack?" Hunter Long, Michael's cousin, asked as they finished hooking a hoist to the bumper of Alexis's car.

Michael had hurriedly excused himself from his mother's house a couple of hours ago, saying he needed to see about Alexis's sedan. Ever since, he'd been trying to think about anything but his mother's suggestion.

He straightened and brushed the mud off his hands by rubbing them together. "There were no vibrations last night. Nor any unmistakable attacks by supernatural beings. I believe my sister-in-law simply found herself in the wrong wash at the wrong time. You know the area is famous for flash floods."

Hunter nodded. "Will she be on the reservation for long? Long enough for explanations?"

Michael shrugged in answer, then turned and waved

at his sister's husband, Junior Gashie. Junior was driving the Navajo Nation's salvage tow truck with a winch and crane that had just been hooked to Alexis's old sedan. From his spot inside the cab, Junior hit the lever, hoisting the rear of the car into position for towing.

Both Junior and Hunter, a Navajo Tribal Police investigator, were covert members of the Brotherhood. Every Brotherhood member had a regular job in addition to his part-time medicine man work with Navajo traditionalists. Few other people on the reservation knew the truth about these men also being warriors for the covert organization.

Michael scrutinized the wreckage as it was lifted into the air. "Not much left to salvage, I'm afraid. I pulled my sister-in-law's luggage out of the trunk. But most of it is ruined."

Hunter nodded. "Water can be deadly." He turned his head to check the area, then turned back to Michael and lowered his voice. "I've decided to return full-time to my job at the tribal police. The Brotherhood has come to a dead end on clues to finding the map.

"We need to capture one of the Skinwalkers alive so we can interrogate him," Hunter continued in a whisper. "Perhaps in my job as investigator, I'll have a better opportunity to manage a capture."

"So far, every Skinwalker we've gotten close to has died before saying anything," Michael reminded him. "I don't think the Navajo Wolf will allow us to capture one of his men alive."

Hunter hunched his shoulders with a frustrated grunt. For months the Brotherhood had been thwarted in their efforts to locate the missing map.

"I need to go back into capture and interrogation," Hunter finally told him. "It's what I do best."

Michael grinned at his cousin. "I'm working on a new strategy. I believe I can find the whereabouts of the ancient Skinwalker parchments without using the lost map. I think the answer we seek lies in the petrographs near the San Juan River and in a few of the old oral legends."

"That would be some project, if you can pull it off."

"Yeah, it'll take at least one assistant and lots of computer time to get the thing done. Have anyone in mind as a helper?"

"Maybe Reagan," Hunter answered. "My sister-in-law, Kody's wife. You know she's a computer whiz."

"Yes, but she also has a toddler at home and another baby on the way. I doubt she has the time this job will take. And everyone else we know has too much work to squeeze in anything extra at the moment." Michael tilted his head in thought. "Perhaps one of my old students at the college will want the extra work."

Hunter shook his head. "It's too dangerous to do that. Any Navajo on the reservation *could* be a Skinwalker in disguise. Don't trust anyone unless you're sure they're not evil—beyond any doubt."

In a distant office, the evil Skinwalker known as the Navajo Wolf slammed his fist down on his desk.

Dammit. The map still eluded him.

With a wheeze and a cough, the Wolf in his human persona sank wearily down into his huge chair. He was barely breathing anymore. The effects of long-term changeovers were increasingly taking his strength and leaving his mind fuzzy.

For nearly a year now, the Skinwalkers had done everything to find the answers they needed to stay alive—to stay in power. But his own body was becoming weaker by the day. The pockmarks across his face and neck had turned to huge craters, announcing exactly who was the evil master of the Skinwalkers to anyone who understood the signs. He'd been forced to stay in his house more and more, scarcely venturing out and having to send lieutenants to do what his own body could no longer handle.

Worst of all was not being able to think.

The only slightly positive thing the Wolf could see in this whole disaster was that the Brotherhood had also been frustrated in their search for the map. What's more, the Skinwalkers now were aware of the names of most of the Brotherhood members. They could keep a closer eye on what each of them was doing.

Still, frustration and growing insanity were surging through the Wolf, bringing a new anger. All his money and knowledge, all his magical power. None of it would keep him or the other Skinwalkers alive. The only possible help for them, the ancient parchments, was buried in a cave somewhere in *Dinetah*.

The Wolf knew his time was running out. A few more weeks or months at the most without help and he would die from the ancient Skinwalker disease. He could already feel himself losing his grip on reality and on the power to change back over to human form.

He had to make sure none of the other Skinwalkers knew just how sick he was. Their greed would make them take advantage of the situation without realizing the sickness would eventually fall on them as well.

What could he do to save himself?

The first thing he intended to do was to stay in human form as long as possible. Maybe that would help for a little while.

What he really needed, though, was to find someone smart enough to figure out the puzzle of where those parchments might be hidden—without using that stupid lost map.

As he thought about finding someone brilliant, a picture came to mind of the Brotherhood professor— what was his name? Oh yes, Michael Ayze. Now there was someone smart enough to figure out where the original Skinwalker had secreted his knowledge of eternal life. Too bad *that* professor was on the wrong side.

The Wolf sat back in his chair and finally had a clear thought. Yes, of course. Why not just let the Brother-hood do his work for him?

With another wheeze, the Wolf reached out trem-bling fingers and grabbed the phone with the hand that still showed long claws from his last change. He would make a call and set his plan in motion.

Lexie tiptoed backwards out of the bedroom, where she'd managed to get her son down for a nap. Jack hadn't wanted to close his eyes; everything had seemed so exciting and new for a four-year-old boy today.

Admittedly, things were certainly different here at his Navajo grandparents' house. But Lexie wasn't so sure she would call what had happened to them so far *thrilling*. Life had taken several crazy and confusing turns the minute they crossed onto the reservation, and she really needed to think about everything that had happened so far.

Fortunately, the house was quiet enough for contemplation this afternoon. Louise had gone to her luncheon. Jack's grandfather Charles, the councilman, had gone to the chapter house for a meeting. And Michael had left hours ago to check on whether her old Volvo sedan could be salvaged.

Thank goodness he'd left when he did. Having him around made it difficult to breathe, let alone to think.

His mother's talk of the two of them getting married in order to maintain an old-fashioned Navajo tradition had actually given Lexie some crazy notions. Notions having less to do with tradition and everything to do with getting her hands on one of the most virile and sexy men she had ever known.

Yikes. Those kinds of thoughts simply had to be buried in her mind for good. It was bad enough that the man seemed to turn her on with just one look. But the very idea of two strangers getting married simply for tradition's sake was causing her to have crazy images.

She fought to remember that first and foremost she was a mother. Jack and his best interests came before everything else—always.

Lexie physically shook the picture of a broad-chested, dark-eyed Navajo man named Michael out of her head as she wandered into the big front room. It was a warm, late September day so no fire had been set in the fireplace. Still, the cozy atmosphere and the soft couches called out to her to come relax into their comfort. Lexie dropped down into overstuffed caramel colored cushions and curled her bare feet up underneath her body.

Michael had said he could get her a job. Fantastic. Just as long as she wouldn't have to work closely with him. Despite Louise's wishes, Lexie knew she couldn't possibly spend a lot of time with the man. Not when her whole body vibrated every time they got near each other.

She needed desperately to think about other things now.

For instance, about how the reservation and the people on it seemed so strange to her. Even in this short time, though, she'd become absolutely convinced her son needed his extended Navajo family—and they needed him. He should learn about his heritage, and it would particularly be in his best interests to form close relationships with his grandparents. Family was all-important.

She would have to have a serious talk with Louise about what had really happened between the family and Dan. Whatever it was didn't seem to extend to her and Jack, so maybe it would be all right.

With her mind racing, Lexie closed her eyes and tried to visualize their lives if they actually stayed on the reservation for the long term. Would Jack end up more Navajo than Anglo? And if he did, wasn't that a good thing?

Perhaps she needed to know a lot more about Navajo traditions before making such an important decision for her child's life. In the meantime, she'd better think about ways of earning the money that would make leaving the reservation possible someday. Just in case.

You can do anything you set your mind to, sweetheart.

Lexie heard an old familiar voice wash over her like a soft caress and opened her eyes to find no one there. Her mother used to make the same comment a lot in her childhood, so often, in fact, it had become part of Lexie's makeup.

Was she daydreaming now? Was she so mixed up with loneliness and new emotions and worry for Jack that she'd been desperate for her mother's voice simply as a friendly echo of a simpler time? Since the horrible day many years ago when she'd learned the truth about her mother's death, Lexie had fought conflicted feelings about having a mother who had taken her own life.

But now…

Lexie closed her eyes again, remembering how badly she'd wanted to talk to her mother one more time. To ask *why*.

She felt a movement and smelled the familiar lavender perfume. "Mommy?" Opening her eyes, she turned to find her mother sitting next to her on the couch.

"It's not crazy being able to see the spirit of someone who can help you in your time of need, Lexie. It's a gift. The gift I left you, which you have always refused to acknowledge."

Lexie opened her mouth to say *take back your damned gift*—she didn't want it. But no words came out. Her mouth just gaped open. Lexie knew very well what was happening to her, but that didn't mean she liked it.

It had always been her *mother's* gift, to see and talk to the spirits of those who had died. And from the day when her mother had died by her own hand, Lexie had sworn never to become involved with such things. She'd tried to bury any hint of the same kind of dreams and had waged a constant battle within herself to remain *normal*.

Now, reaching a shaky hand outward, Lexie was afraid…though not of her mother. Not even of seeing ghosts in general. No, she was petrified that the vision would disappear in a puff of smoke, and then she wouldn't get to ask the questions that had haunted her for most of her life.

The vision took her hand. "It's okay, sweetie. I have come here to help you."

To hear her mother using the same endearment with her that she used with Jack was like having cold water thrown over her head. Lexie finally found her voice. "Mom, am I crazy now, too? Like you were? Is that what you've come to tell me?

"Not at all, baby." Her mother smiled, and Lexie found herself sighing over the way the corners of mother's eyes crinkled up the way she remembered.

"It's important that *someone* can hear—and know," her mother said cryptically. "*You* are the one with the sight now, and I'm only here to help you listen and hear."

The ghost of her mother chuckled and shrugged. "I guess it doesn't really matter what any of us thinks we want. Sorry, sweetie. We all do what we are meant to do."

"I don't want you." Lexie found more than her voice. She found an old anger, one that had been building for twenty years. "You left me. You took the easy way out of your problems and left Dad and me all by ourselves. Go away now and leave me and my son alone."

"I'm sorry, Lexie," her mother said with a catch in her voice. "I stayed for your sake as long as I could. But I was weaker than you are. You're so much stronger than I could ever be, and you always have been.

"I really never meant to hurt you, my love."

A part of Lexie wanted badly to believe her mother's words. To find a way of letting go of the anger. But she couldn't imagine any situation where she would simply give in and accept the visions without a fight.

"I've been summoned here by spirits of the Navajo to help you learn to listen," her mother continued. "They need your help. They need your strength."

"They do? But how on earth can I do anything for them? It's all I can manage to help Jack and myself."

"The Navajo people have evil living amongst them. Evil they cannot see."

"*Evil?* Then maybe I should take Jack and leave."

"Jack is in no danger. Your son is exactly where he belongs. His Navajo blood and his *Dine* clan will protect him."

"Mom, you're scaring me now. Is your job to frighten me?" There had always been a part of Lexie that had both hated and loved her mother. She might be willing to believe anything at this point.

"Not at all. I know you're conflicted." Her mother reached over soothingly and patted the hand still holding hers. "I've only come to ask you to remain open and to learn. There is someone on this side who has a message for the *Dine*. You must deliver the message. But they tell me you won't understand unless you learn about the Way."

"But how…"

"Listen to Michael Ayze. He offers both answers and protection. Soon you will get the opportunity to return his kindness. Most of the Navajo people don't even know they are in need. But you can be the one to help them."

The mere mention of Michael made Lexie start to

sweat. She dragged her hand from her mother's and closed her eyes again. She visualized him standing over her in the rain, offering his strength and watching her with those penetrating and arrogant brown eyes.

Suddenly the image in her mind changed, grew watery and indistinct. She thought she could hear someone breathing heavily in the darkness. Something was after her. Her heart beat wildly, thundering in her chest.

This was nuts. Only a bad dream. Lexie forced open her eyes, fully expecting to see her mother next to her. But the figure sitting beside her on the couch now was not her mother.

The dark image of an older Navajo man sat next to her, studying her with black eyes. His face was creased, and the jowls under his chin resembled a mean bulldog's more than a real man's. Lexie gasped for breath and scooted back, trying to put as much space between her and this unearthly vision as possible.

"Where's my mom? Who are you?" she managed at last.

The creepy, demonic figure said nothing. But he reached out with strong, fat fingers and grabbed her hand.

"Stop it. Let go of me." Lexie was beginning to panic. Oh Lord. She was in big trouble here.

He forced open her fisted hand and placed something small and smooth into her palm. Automatically, she closed her fingers over it and ripped her hand from his in self-defense.

She had to protect herself, but the small, smooth objects he'd put into her hand were not much in the way of a defensive weapon, whatever they were. The very real beginnings of hysteria were making her unable to think. Closing her eyes against the onslaught of terrible panic, she curled her body into a tight ball and started to whimper.

"Come on, Alexis. Easy now. You're having a bad dream. It's okay." Michael sat beside her and touched her shoulder.

She jerked open her eyes and fell into his out-stretched arms. He caught her and tried to soothe her as she burrowed into his broad chest.

"The man," she whimpered. "Like a bad dog. Only really evil. Dark. He wanted—"

"Nothing. It was only a dream." Michael placed a soft kiss against her hair and rocked her in his arms.

When he'd come into his parents' front room and found her on the couch crying in her sleep, his heart had stood still. Now he felt her body trembling as she clung to him.

He pulled her into his lap. "I'm here. You're safe. That must have been some nightmare."

She moved restlessly against him. "It was real. I've fought against this for most of my life. But I couldn't stop it this time. I...you won't believe me."

"Shush." He tipped her chin up so she could see his face, see how concerned he was for her welfare. "Relax a minute. If it still feels real and not like a dream after a few minutes, then tell me. I promise I'll believe whatever you say."

She looked up at him, her eyes dark and unfocused in what seemed like lingering terror. Then she sighed and rested her head against his shoulder. He felt a shudder run through her body, and the immediate effect on him was devastating.

He'd been afraid of this. The desire to protect her was urgent and overwhelming. He wanted to help her. More. He wanted to possess her. He thought he'd buried these unwanted feelings years ago, yet within twenty-four hours of her arrival, they were back as strong as ever.

Dammit. He'd pictured himself as a solitary man, and imagined that's just the way things were supposed to be for him. But he wanted this woman—both her body and spirit.

He cursed himself for the bad timing. For the bad choice of woman. There was nothing right about the whole thing. But there you had it. He was desperate to make love to his brother's widow.

Lifting his head, he held his breath. He didn't want to scare her. Things must seem so different here in *Dinetah* to her. Add in the fact her brother-in-law was a lust-crazed idiot, and it might just send her away for good.

But it didn't mean he still couldn't protect her. Befriend her.

"Don't leave." She jerked her head up.

"I'm right here." As he said the words, he felt her body relax.

"I have to tell you about my background before what just happened to me will make any sense to you."

"All right. I'm listening."

"My mother…committed suicide when I was eight. She'd been born with a gift, the ability to see spirits. And it became too much for her to live with."

"Spirits? Like dead people?" Of all the things on

earth he had thought she might tell him, this was the very last thing he would ever have imagined.

Watching him carefully through those amazing, misty hazel eyes, Alexis nodded her head. "When I was little, my mother told me about having the *sight* and said she would train me to see ghosts, too. That I had to accept such things as my heritage."

"Did her abilities scare you? Did you consider what she told you a threat?"

"Not at all. I thought it might be fun to see ghosts, even though my father warned me my mother's ability made her weak and unhappy. He didn't particularly want me to become involved. But he wouldn't have stopped me."

Alexis took a deep breath. He noticed she had both hands fisted as if ready to fight for her visions, and he knew telling this was costing her something. He tightened his grip on her shoulders.

"With maturity, I've realized my mother's gift wasn't the only thing that drove her to take her own life. She had many demons. But being so different, so odd, was the final problem that put her over the edge of sanity."

"I'm sorry."

Shrugging, she gave him the slightest crack of a smile. "I'm not a confused little girl anymore. My father loved me enough for both of them. And I loved him enough to put any potential visions of my own aside. I refused to allow any *spirits* into my world from her death forward. And I've managed to hold them off ever since."

Her chest heaved in a tremendous sigh. "Until now."

"You mean you weren't dreaming, but talking to dead people? Here? In my parents' living room?"

Michael glanced around, felt the chill and wondered how to help her. "That's not something I would discuss with anyone else you might meet in *Dinetah*."

"Huh?"

"On the reservation. This land the *Dine* consider sacred."

"Oh. Here. Yeah, I imagine you probably think I'm insane. But what I told you is true." She set her chin and pursed her lips.

He heard her disappointment in him, watched her struggle with the words to make him understand. "I know dreams can sometimes seem very real," he tried in a soothing tone. "Tell me about them."

She scowled up at him. He couldn't stop himself from rubbing his thumb gently over the wrinkles she'd created in that gorgeous face.

Pushing his hand away, she narrowed her eyes at him. "Aren't you the one who is interested in research? I'll tell you what I learned from the visions, but only if you promise to keep an open mind."

He crossed a hand over his chest. "I promise."

"Well, first of all, I spoke to my mother. She was sitting right where you are now."

"The same mother who committed suicide was here?"

Her frown deepened. "Right. She said she came to tell me the Navajo people need me. I'm supposed to learn stuff from you so I can help them."

"You mean learn things about the Navajo Way, like my mother mentioned?" He'd thought Alexis wouldn't go along with his mother's suggestions. Maybe she was trying to tell him she'd changed her mind.

"I wanted to ask more questions. But..." She hesitated and her eyes grew dark again. "But then something terrible—a horrible image came out of nowhere and grabbed me."

"What? Are you hurt?" He rubbed his hands up and down her arms, trying to judge if she was in any pain.

"No. Just scared. The image appeared to be an older Native American man. Navajo I suppose. But the vision was all watery and dark. In fact, the man kind of resembled a big dog instead of a real person."

"An animal?" Such a dream was an extremely bad omen for her to have in his world. "That must've been one nasty nightmare."

"It wasn't a nightmare. I told you, I really saw him." Lexie reared back and shoved her closed fist up toward his face where he could see it. "I can prove it. The very real nightmare gave me something. Look."

When she opened her fingers to show him, Michael was stunned to see small objects he clearly recognized in her palm. *Bone beads.*

Swearing in Navajo, Michael fought his instinct to run.

What the devil was going on here? *Bone beads were the sign of the Skinwalkers!*

Chapter 4

"Give those to me," he demanded.

Lexie closed her fist, not willing to give an inch. "Well, don't look so horrified. It was me who saw ghosts, not you."

She watched as Michael's face ran through a gamut of expressions. Within seconds, his mouth softened and his eyes took on a slightly superior edge. The look on his face had become the mirror image of one of her professors back at college. It was easy to tell what he did for a living.

"Let me explain about *Dine* beliefs," he said authoritatively.

"Dine?"

"The People. Navajo."

She nodded in understanding.

"The *Dine* believe that when someone dies, their

spirits, both good and bad, are released to the world with their last dying breath. The bad spirits are called *chindi* and they're the evil forces that stick around after death to avenge some offense. The *good* spirits, or winds, inside a person quickly disperse to join the universal harmony.

"You can understand then why we don't buy into the idea of helpful ghosts," he added. "If they're here, they're evil. And no one wants such things inside their homes."

"I sort of understand, but…"

"The bone beads in your hand are an infinitely worse sign than mere ghosts, however. Bone beads mean witchcraft. And witchcraft is a complete reversal of the Navajo Way."

"Witchcraft? You don't believe in the possibility of seeing *friendly* ghosts, but you do believe in evil spirits and witches? You're joking."

"Not at all," he said with a scowl. "The People have lived with the knowledge of witches throughout their history. They exist today. And the fact that the evil spirit you claim you saw resembled a dog makes things all the more difficult for you.

"There is ancient evil alive on the rez today, Alexis," he continued after a pause. "Malevolent witches who are known as Skinwalkers and can turn themselves into various forms, appearing as apparitions of the wolf, raven, snake, owl, bear…and a huge wild dog."

"Like…like the man I saw in my vision?"

Michael narrowed his eyes to study her. "Exactly like that."

"You actually believe shape-shifters exist in real life?"

"Unfortunately, yes. I know the Skinwalkers are real

and extremely dangerous. I've seen them with my own eyes."

He probably shouldn't be considered crazy to believe in such things. After all, *she* was the one who saw dead people.

Michael appeared to be perfectly sane. But to believe in real shape-shifters… Heaven help them if what he said turned out to be true. Was this the evil Dan and her mother had warned her about?

"Those beads in your hand are a terrible thing to bring into a traditional Navajo home," Michael told her gently. "You have committed a sacrilege, one that will take a curing ceremony to fix."

"But I didn't bring them here. I didn't even know they were evil."

"You need to know. If you intend to stay in Navajo-land for any time, you must learn about such things."

"Okay," she said with frustration in her voice. "I agree with that. But if you're to be the one to teach me, you'll have to learn about my heritage, too. It appears I can't help who I am any more than you can help what you believe."

He took a deep breath. "Fine. Now give me those taboo objects."

"Gladly." She dumped the beads into his palm. "I have to go check on my son." Lexie jumped up and made her way down the hallway toward the bedrooms.

After she was out of sight, Michael pulled his medicine pouch from its place on his belt and prepared a quick blessing to halt the transmission of evil spirits coming from the beads. Later he would burn and bury them as prescribed by tradition.

He tried to focus on Alexis's tale of the visions, but

he kept coming back to the look in her eyes as she was telling him the story. She believed in every fantastic thing she had told him. More than that, it was as though she'd been primed and ready to accept the witchcraft concept when he'd turned the tables and told her about the Skinwalkers.

His skin crawled at the thought of real Skinwalkers coming right into his family's home. Could they do that through Lexie's visions?

He could barely think straight. His emotions were already unsettled. And had been ever since last night when he first laid eyes on Alexis after all these years.

He'd fought hard to maintain his distance when she'd appeared in *Dinetah*. Nevertheless, he'd been drawn to her side.

For the last few years, as the Skinwalker war raged across *Dinetah,* any kind of desire had been the last thing on his mind. But Alexis had kindled some long buried flame the minute she'd come into his world. He'd never met a woman with such an elegant—yet sensual manner—about her. The conflict of wanting to know the woman underneath was driving him nuts.

Those very same internal conflicts had kept him away from his brother over their entire married life. He'd been afraid of being around her. She was his brother's wife, out of bounds. And now she was his brother's widow and the mother of his child. Still out of bounds.

Watching the way she treated her son, with such tenderness and ferocious care, had unfortunately only made him want her more. It seemed to him that a mother tiger lurked within the beautiful but fragile shell of

Alexis Ayze. Such an idea was more than a little appealing.

And damned if his own canny mother hadn't somehow picked up on his feelings. There was no way she would've come up with those old *Dine* marriage traditions so casually if she hadn't already realized he felt something toward Alexis.

Like most of the *Dine* who tried to live as tradition dictated, his mother was constantly torn between new and old. She drove a car, used electric heat and air-conditioning in her house and was in many ways a modern working woman. Yet at the same time, she fought hard to convince herself she was living as a tradition-based Navajo who followed in the footsteps of her ancestors.

Still, his mother's motivation where he and Alexis were concerned was obvious. Louise Ayze did indeed want her oldest son married and settled. Hadn't she been nagging him since he'd returned to *Dinetah* to find a nice woman? But Louise's biggest reason to insist on a traditional union between him and his Anglo sister-in-law was even more basic—keeping her grandson Jack near by.

Michael had almost convinced himself he needed to send Alexis away. For both of their sakes. But now that she'd been accosted by a Skinwalker, even if it was the *ghost* of a Skinwalker, he couldn't leave her alone. He didn't dare let her out of his sight. His life would be less than worthless if anything happened to her because he was afraid to be close.

His thoughts turned to the Skinwalker spirit she'd supposedly seen. Why had it come to her at his parents' house?

Their home had been blessed with a special

ceremony to ward off Skinwalkers. So if it turned out the evil ones had found a way to break in anyway, then the Brotherhood could be in for terror like they'd never seen before.

On the other hand, to be fair to Alexis, the People had never been able to keep all *chindi* out of a house—blessed or not. Not when a person could die at any time. In the old days, the *Dine* would sometimes abandon a hogan when a death had accidentally occurred inside. Back then they believed the evil *chindi* would be trapped there forever.

Today, the modern People preferred to take their ill relatives to the hospital to die. Or they had ceremonies and special traditions for restoring a house and those within it to harmony in case death came suddenly.

If what Alexis had seen were merely ghostly spirits, it might not be as bad as if live Skinwalkers were trying to take over her mind. The regular sort of evil spirit could potentially be sent away with the right cure.

But the real question for him now was why. Why had a Skinwalker *chindi* come to Alexis at all? And why come here?

Michael shook his head. Too many confusing questions.

He needed time to think. Time for his brain to come up with a few decent answers. For now his only choice was to go through the motions. Protect his family and find ways to stay near Alexis for her protection. That's all he could do until things became clearer.

Lexie touched Jack's forehead and found it cool. He looked so peaceful. Fluffing her fingers through his hair, she sat down next to her son's bed and watched him sleep. Oh, to be four again and be able to rest so soundly.

She tucked her knees up under her chin, wrapped her arms around her legs and sighed. Jack was her whole life. What would be the best thing for him?

Unfortunately, she didn't have a lot of choices. The reason she'd brought him to the reservation in the first place was they had run out of money. That hadn't changed. Now she didn't even have the use of her car, so leaving at all would be tough.

But if she truly thought her child was in danger, she would find a way. She would borrow the money and take a bus if necessary. But a bus to where? Would anywhere in the world be safer for Jack than with his extended family?

No, she was absolutely convinced Jack was where he belonged. There was love here for him. Love and learning—and understanding. She desperately wanted all of those things for her boy.

Her mind switched back to the safety issue. Was her son safe? Lexie wasn't nearly as sure about that.

She looked down at his sleeping form and caught the remnants of a tiny smile on his lips. Her gut instincts screamed for her to let him stay right here. She tried to reason it through, but instead kept having flashes of her mother's ghostly image.

Her mother's spirit had claimed Jack was safe here, but she hadn't said anything about Lexie being safe, too. What if it was only her who might be in danger on the reservation? Would the trouble maybe bounce off her and go right back to her son?

Such scary thoughts brought a tiny bubble of distress

to her lips. Was it possible that her son might be better off without her?

"Mommy?" Jack stirred awake and reached out toward her. "Are we okay?"

Lexie pulled him up and into her lap. "We're fine, honey." So far. "Let's get your shoes on, wash your face and go see what we can find in your grandmother's kitchen for a snack."

By the time Lexie and Jack got to the kitchen, Louise Ayze had returned from her luncheon.

"Well, good afternoon, you two. Look what I have for you," she said to Jack with a wide beam. Louise handed him a banana and a clear plastic bag full of Goldfish crackers.

"How'd you guess those are Jack's favorite foods?"

"No need to guess. It's what his father and uncle liked best when they were his age."

Lexie could see the love shining in her mother-in-law's eyes. How could Jack be in any trouble with so much goodwill surrounding him?

She settled her son at the kitchen table with his treats and his electronic learning game then looked around, but saw no sign of Michael.

"If you are seeking my eldest son, he is performing *hataalii* duties in the medicine hogan out behind the house."

"I've heard you use that term before. *Hataalii*," she tried to pronounce it the same way as Louise had. "What's it mean?"

Louise pointed to a chair at the far end of the table. "Sit with me, Daughter. I will explain."

After pouring them both a glass of iced tea, Louise sat down beside her. "*Hataalii* is the *Dine* word for medicine man. I told you last night that to be a traditional Navajo means to maintain balance—staying in harmony within and without your natural body. But there is always the potential for disorder in life. When bad things happen, the medicine man uses a variety of methods, mostly through our various ceremonies, to make things right."

"What kind of methods do you mean?" Lexie had visions of dangerous and weird rituals.

"The medicine men use herbs, prayers, songs and sand drawings in their ceremonies. A qualified medicine man is a unique individual given supernatural powers to diagnose a person's problem and also to heal or cure illness by restoring harmony."

Well, those sorts of things didn't sound too bad. But supernatural powers? She'd have to think that over.

"We were blessed when our son accepted his calling and went through the many years of training necessary to become a *hataalii.* He learned the ceremonies from his maternal great-uncle, a famous and experienced traditional medicine man.

"Indeed," Louise continued after a breath, "our oldest child has grown into a man who would be any woman's idea of a well-respected husband."

Uh-oh. "Where did you say Michael was now?"

"All traditional families keep a medicine hogan nearby. It's the round house I pointed out to you this morning on the way down to the barn. Every ceremony is performed in them—even weddings."

Just then Jack's grandfather came in and offered to

take Jack back down to the corral to see the horse. Lexie jumped at the chance to escape her mother-in-law for a few minutes and volunteered to accompany them outside.

She badly needed to talk to Michael before she spent any more time with Louise. Shape-shifters, ghosts, medicine men and arranged marriages. Yikes.

What could Lexie possibly say to a woman who had such confusing beliefs?

"I don't know what else to say to you, my mother." Michael was frustrated by trying to find ways of telling his mother about Alexis's *chindi* ghosts without throwing her ingrained sense of natural order right out the window.

He'd come back to the house after dealing with the bone beads. And since finding his mother alone in the house, he'd been attempting to prepare her for what was to come.

Standing in her kitchen, waiting for his father to bring Alexis and Jack back inside for dinner, Michael had been trying to find a way to make his mother accept his newest decisions without giving her all the details and scaring her too much.

He took a breath and tried to become the competent *hataalii* she expected him to be. "I can tell you no more than that Alexis has had a disturbing dream and I've decided this home needs a cure. I've called and asked your son-in-law to perform the ceremony. And in return, he's invited you and my father to stay with your daughter for a few days while he completes the blessing."

"Will this be a Blessing Way ceremony?" Louise

asked. "That would normally mean the entire clan should be invited, and food should be prepared. And if it is, why will we have to move out of our home for four days? Please explain."

Michael decided to exert his influence as a medicine man. "Mother, do you question my ceremonial decisions?"

"No, of course not. I just don't understand the need for…"

He gently took her hand. "I promise it's for the best. There *is* a need for this house to be cured, and I've taken steps to see it will be done right.

"Think of the time you'll be away as a vacation." He grinned at his mother and saw her expression soften. "You aren't going too far, only over to my sister's home."

Junior's wife and Michael's sister, Naomi, and her young family lived in a new house, built nearby on her maternal clan's grazing lease land. Within walking distance of her mother's home. It was the traditional Navajo Way.

"What about my daughter-in-law and grandson? Will they have to leave this house, too?"

"I think it would be a good idea for Jack to meet his cousins. It'll be fun for him to go with you and stay with them for a while. But…" How on earth was he going to word this next part to keep her from jumping to false conclusions?

"And what about your future wife?"

Yep. That was exactly the kind of conclusion he'd been trying to avoid. "A marriage between Alexis and I is not at all settled, Mother." He watched his mother's eyebrows lift. As far as she was concerned, the subject was closed.

No use arguing about it. In fact, the rest of what he had to say would probably please his mother very much.

"I've decided Alexis should become my research assistant. I'm in the middle of a complicated anthropology project and I'll need her with me constantly. So I believe she should stay in my guest room for the duration of the project.

"You should be very happy about my decision." Michael continued in his *good son* voice. "The time we spend together will give both of us a chance to get to know each other better. And, of course, it'll give me the opportunity to begin her lessons in the *Dine* traditions."

"Alexis has agreed to all of this?" his mother asked. "Agreed to leaving her son in our care and stay with you?" She could barely keep the joy out of her eyes.

"*If* she agrees," Michael continued, "I'll make sure she sees Jack at least once a day."

"I would expect my daughter-in-law to already know her son will be secure in his aunt's home and safe being watched by his grandmother," that very grandmother announced. "She should not have to worry. I will speak to her."

Yeah, Michael figured that would clinch it. Alexis was as powerless around his meddling and overbearing mother as all the rest of the clan.

Lexie's head was spinning. When she and Jack and her father-in-law had walked back into the house from the barn, Louise had been a whirlwind in motion. The tiny woman was packing up the refrigerator and issuing orders for everyone else to pack their clothes and bathroom items.

Pulling Michael aside, Lexie tried to find out what was going on. "What happened?"

"It was the only way I could think of to get everyone out of the house so the damage caused by the bone beads can be repaired," Michael said as he dragged her down the hallway and out of earshot.

"The whole family has to move to your sister's house? But it's so disruptive." Lexie took a breath. "This is all my fault."

"Not at all. You didn't invite the ghost of the Skinwalker to come here, did you?"

She shook her head. "But is there room for everyone over there at your sister's?"

Michael's facial expression took a suspicious turn. Quite unlike the usual egotistical and macho manner she expected from him, his gaze now skittered away from hers, landing absently on dead space over her shoulder.

"You and I won't be staying there." His voice was casual, the sound hoarse. "But we'll help get everyone settled tonight. Naomi has even volunteered to help you rebuild your and Jack's lost wardrobes with some of their clothing. She's about your size—"

"Wait," Lexie cut in. She'd caught the obvious discrepancies in what he'd left out. "Slow down. Are you saying your parents and Jack will be staying with your sister's family but you and I will not?"

A slice of panic over her child's welfare left her breathless. Breathing through her nose, she fought to remain calm and tried to steel herself.

"Alexis, stop a moment and—"

"Will he be safe?" she interrupted. "Really safe?"

Michael nodded grimly. "Remember, it's you who's brought the *chindi* into the house. Have you considered the possibility that staying too close to you might prove more dangerous for Jack than being out of your sight?"

As a matter of fact, she had thought of it. Sighing, she shrugged a shoulder and blinked her eyes to stem the growing tears.

"But he's just a baby," she whispered.

Michael stood silently, arms dropped at his sides and watched her struggle with both her gut instincts and her maternal sixth sense. Finally, she gave in to what she knew was inevitable.

"I suppose you're right." Lexie turned her face, hiding her gaze from Michael's concerned stare. "Will I have to stay away from him for very long, do you think?"

Michael reached out and pulled her closer. "I know how hard this is for you. But you're being very strong."

Lexie dropped her head against his chest. She didn't feel strong. She felt all weak and wobbly. But the safety she felt here, in the warmth and circle of Michael arms, gave her the strength she needed to stay on her feet.

"Don't worry so much," he whispered against her hair. "My mother will make sure Jack is well cared for and happy. And I promise you can either see him or call him every day."

Michael's heartbeat picked up speed right then, and a new tension seemed to run from him to her, heading down her spine to her core. She didn't understand why she'd suddenly started noticing how small she felt standing there beside him. Or why it had just dawned on her that his big, really big shoulders felt as if they sheltered her from any potential evil.

But those big arms and bigger shoulders were also deviling her with out-of-place sensual sensations. Whatever forces between them had caused a change in the air were also beginning to make her feel itchy and hot.

He cleared his throat, took her gently by the shoulders and held her an arm's length away. "Any time you want to change the plan, just say the word. It would kill me and my family to lose you two now we've just found you. But when you decide to take Jack and leave the reservation, I'll gladly give you the money to help you on your way."

He was being too damned nice. She couldn't stand it. She would leave someday. But not yet.

"I…" She had to clear her own raspy throat and also take a step back. "What if Jack is scared or doesn't want to be separated from me? He's never been on his own before."

"Let's hear what Jack has to say after he meets his cousins and sees where he'll be staying."

"Really, Mommy? I get to spend the night with Emily and Teddy? And all their horses and ponies? All by myself?" Jack looked a little too excited at the prospect of getting away from Mommy for a while.

Her son was growing up, trying to find his path to independence. That was good, wasn't it? The way things were supposed to be in a child's development.

But her heart took a big dip at the thought of her baby not needing her anymore. Her first impulse was to bait him into saying he would miss her terribly and would rather she stayed close.

Instead, Lexie took a deep breath and forced a smile. There really was little choice.

"You'll have a terrific time," she told him as her eyes began to cloud over. "And your grandmother and grandfather will be here, too. It'll be like a big party."

"Okay." Jack pulled away from her and turned, ready to run to find his cousins again.

She hooked his arm and spun him back, planting a big kiss on his lips. "You be good. I'll see you tomorrow."

Jack used his sleeve to wipe her kiss from his mouth, but nodded at her. "Okay, Mommy. I'll be good."

She wanted to grab him up and keep a hold on him forever. But she let him go.

"See you," he called over his shoulder as he pounded down the hall toward his cousins' bedrooms.

"Yeah," she whispered past the sob building in her throat. "I love you, baby. And I'll see you soon."

Lexie had managed to do the right thing. The only thing she could.

Chapter 5

The Skinwalker who could change from his human form and become the Burrowing Owl entered his boss's office. Trying to hide his true feelings, the Owl prepared himself to answer to the ridiculous and sick witchman—his boss, the Navajo Wolf.

The Owl wished he and his allies were ready to overthrow the Wolf and take charge of the Skinwalkers. But he soothed his ruffled feathers with the knowledge it would not be too long. A few more months at the most and his forces would be in place and prepared to go. The armies loyal to the Wolf were dwindling. The forces loyal to him were growing.

"I demand to know your progress on obtaining the map," the Wolf growled.

The Owl wasn't terribly concerned about locating the Wolf's map. However, he would continue going through the motions to keep the Wolf from guessing his true intentions. When he did find the map, the priceless relic was going to be *his*, not the Wolf's. But by then the Wolf wouldn't need it anyway. The dead seldom cared about maps or parchments.

The Owl felt it would be beneficial to his cause if he could confuse the Wolf by giving him a lame excuse. "The Brotherhood professor, Michael Ayze, has not returned from his leave of absence. He's been unreachable."

"I told you to stay with him," the Wolf argued with a snarl. "You're reputed to be almost as smart as he is. Use your intelligence to learn what he's up to."

The Owl clenched his teeth and kept a calm demeanor. "I have one of your best men, the Bear, watching him—as close by as he dares. But it seems your brilliant Professor Ayze has a new diversion. An Anglo woman has recently arrived in Navajoland, and apparently she has become the new object of his entire focus."

The Wolf looked perplexed. His watery eyes lost some of their evil luster.

Finally, the Wolf muttered, "Nonsense. That enemy brainiac has always been centered and single-minded. I know his type. He's determined to best the Skinwalkers through intelligence alone."

The Wolf laughed at the idea of anyone beating him with mere brain power. "Stay with our friend Professor Ayze. Have your men get closer to him and be ready. He will either find the map or go straight for the parchments very soon now. When he does, I want whatever he finds. And then I want him dead."

"But the woman—"

The Wolf gave a weak wave of his hand. "If he

spends too long absorbed with the female, get rid of her. Nothing can be allowed to stand in the way."

Michael chanced a glance toward Alexis, who was sitting in the front passenger seat of his truck. "You okay?"

It was late, but they were only driving the ten-mile stretch between his sister's house and his own. Since they'd started out a few minutes ago, Michael had been secretly listening for the Skinwalker buzz—just in case. So far, all was quiet.

Heaving a big sigh, Alexis said, "Yeah. I've been sitting here reminding myself that if I'd had enough money to get a job at home, I would've had to enroll Jack in day care or preschool so I could go to work. So leaving him with his cousins and grandparents seems like a much better option for both of us."

"A very intelligent thought."

He heard her wry laugh through the darkness. "Right. I'm a genius." She fidgeted in her seat. "I suppose it's not having him with me at night that's getting me down the most. He's never been tucked in to bed by anyone else."

"Alexis, let me…" He raised his hand to pat her on the shoulder, but withdrew it before he made contact.

He knew she was hurting and he wanted desperately to take her in his arms for comfort. But it had been difficult enough just sitting beside her like this. Michael wished he had the nerve and inner strength left at the moment to touch her as a friend would. But he didn't. Couldn't.

"Please call me *Lexie*," she broke in, saving him from finishing a sentence that should never have been started. "Alexis seems so formal. Now that we're going to be working together I think we should try to be comfortable with each other."

Comfortable. Not a word or concept he would've chosen. "All right. If you wish." The two of them must be crazy to attempt anything like this.

"But don't call me Lex, please. That's the nickname Dan used, and I always hated it."

Michael could think of several endearing names he would like to call her. But calling such an elegant and feminine woman *Lex* would never have entered his mind.

"One of our old *Dine* traditions requires us to refrain from using a person's given name when speaking directly to them and when speaking about them to others," he told her. "The idea is that doing so diminishes their power. Most traditional People are given nicknames as children or they go by their relationship names. Like *daughter* or *son.*"

Lexie looked interested in this discussion of tradition. "You mean something like me not calling Louise by her given name and calling her Mother instead?"

"Yes, exactly. Perhaps I'll try to come up with another nickname for you." Whenever he could actually think clearly again.

They rode in silence the rest of the way to his house. After he helped her inside with the few things he'd salvaged from her car and the clothes and shoes Naomi had given her, he showed her around his place.

Lexie kept her mouth shut and just nodded while Michael pointed out where the bedrooms and bathroom were located. She wasn't sure what to say to him that wouldn't bring her more trouble. So she just memorized the room layouts and prepared herself to be a good assistant.

When they peeked into what he'd called his *office,* she saw more books than had been in the public library back in Louisiana. "Wow. Lots of books on your shelves. Have you read them all?"

She didn't want to mention the dozens of messy files stacked on his desk, on the floor and beside the chair. They were in contrast to the rest of the house which seemed spotless. He must really need an assistant.

Michael smiled at her, and once more she was struck by his high brow and the sharp cheekbones. Here was an intelligent man with a strong chin and penetrating eyes—and one very uncharacteristic messy streak.

But even with the single bad habit, Michael was much stronger in both body and mind than his brother ever had been. She let her gaze drop to his wide, full mouth, and all her senses snapped to attention, captured totally by the sight of sensual lips and a crooked, masculine smile. He didn't remind her of her late husband at all. Not even one little bit.

Lexie suddenly felt more tired than she'd ever been and turned away from the sight of him. There had been too many emotions and sensations for her mind to endure in the last twenty-four hours. And in her weakened condition she had no intention of remaining this close to a compelling temptation in the form of one sexy-as-hell brother-in-law who was now her boss. It was all she could do to be civil and not turn tail and run for her life.

"Most of the books in here are for study," he told her with a smile in his voice. "But currently I have a home computer hooked to the Internet by satellite, and I use the books less for reference."

"Reference for what?" she asked around a yawn she'd barely managed to conceal.

"Anthropology projects. You'll find out all about it tomorrow when we get started. But for tonight, I think you'd better get some sleep. It looks like you can barely stand on your own two feet anymore."

"I'm not—" She interrupted herself with a full fledged and embarrassing yawn.

"Shall I carry you to bed?" There were coppery edges to his words, as if he'd deliberately said them with a double meaning.

Oh man, the images his words conjured up almost undid her resolve to stay away from him. "No, thanks." Her own words came out much more raspy and tentative than she'd meant.

He lifted his eyebrows and pursed his lips as if he wondered what had made her voice so sketchy. But the twinkle in his eyes let her know he hadn't missed a thing.

"I remember where the guest bedroom is," she hurriedly added. "I'll just show myself there right now if it's all the same to you."

"Fine. Sleep well. I'll see you tomorrow."

Lexie dashed out of the room without another word. Making her way down the hall, she tried to get a grip on her senses.

Michael Ayze was her brother-in-law, her host for a few days, and as of tomorrow he would be her boss. Why was he also the absolutely sexiest man she had ever met?

The sound of his low, sensual voice was making her drool. The extraordinary sight of his eyes flaming whenever he looked in her direction left her weak in the knees.

Yet the man couldn't be more out of bounds. She had plenty of problems without adding the complications of having an affair with Michael. As a single mother, a woman in desperate need of a job and longing for a loving family for her child, she needed to keep her cool. It was bad enough that she felt totally out of her element on the reservation and was apparently sliding headfirst into weird paranormal quicksand.

So how was she ever going to live through working beside him?

After a couple of hours of tossing and turning and not being able to get Lexie out of his mind, Michael rolled out of bed and went to sit alone on his back deck. For as long as he could remember, he'd been enamored with the way the stars always seemed to cocoon his traditional world on a clear night in *Dinetah*.

Most traditional Navajos stayed inside after dark. But not him. There was nothing that gave him more peace than watching the night skies and listening to the critters who populated the darkness.

Noncloudy nights in late summer and early fall were the best times to experience the ancient blanket of the cosmos. The air was clear, the constellations in crisp relief against a velvet sky.

Tonight the planets and supernovas were especially spectacular as they inched across the skies. Even so, he had barely noticed them. His mind had been lost in the stars appearing in a pair of gentle hazel eyes.

Propping up his feet on the wooden railing, Michael

wanted to use his normal scientific analysis in an effort to figure out what was causing him to lose concentration. There must be some valid reason why nothing but Lexie made any sense to him tonight.

He came to the conclusion that maybe his body had been reacting to Lexie with such a testosterone rush for one simple and completely natural reason—because it'd been such a damned long time since he'd had any woman. Thinking back, he realized he'd been living through at least a couple of years of celibacy. What with the Skinwalker war and the Brotherhood's original vow of celibacy, and more recently his consuming anthropology work, time had flown by and he hadn't really noticed. Until now.

No wonder he was feeling horny as hell around a woman as sensual as Lexie. Such a thing would be natural for any male.

Natural maybe, but not something he intended to indulge in now. Time to put a stop to thinking with the wrong body part. He shifted uncomfortably in his seat.

Now if only he could convince his rebellious body to go along with his mind. She wasn't stupid. She would easily guess what was happening with him the minute she caught a glimpse of the constant rock hardness lurking behind his jeans' zipper. Dammit.

The first hint of predawn light captured his attention just then, and made him remember he was supposed to be thinking of more important considerations than the natural release of his urges. Nothing was going to happen between him and Lexie. A relationship made up of anything more than friendship or boss-employee loyalty was *not* a possibility.

Besides that, years ago he'd come to the conclusion that sex for sex's sake was not for him. When he held a woman close, it was because they both wanted to be there, in a lasting relationship. Love, respect and loyalty were the things which made a coupling the most satisfying.

And none of those things was going to happen between him and Lexie. Well, except for the loyalty maybe. But she wouldn't be staying on the reservation once she had the money to leave. And he belonged here and had vowed never to walk away from his homeland again. Love and respect would probably take years to develop between two people as different as they were.

So, he might as well suck up some desperately needed resolve and get over wanting her. It was time to return to his own reality and quit dreaming about long silky legs, high perky breasts and a tight sassy butt. He was old enough and wise enough to know better. Or at least he tried to tell himself he was.

At the moment what Michael really needed to concentrate on was getting a handle on Lexie's ghost sightings. She'd said such things had never happened to her before she arrived on the reservation, despite the fact her mother had talked to ghosts when she'd been alive. If that was true, then why here?

Were the Skinwalkers somehow using her to get to him? Maybe they foresaw a way to slow down the Brotherhood through her—the same way they had used women in the past.

Michael shook his head. The idea didn't have much merit when it came to Lexie. He couldn't imagine what the Skinwalkers would want with an Anglo woman who had no money and no power. Michael also believed he was too smart to allow anything to stand in the way of ridding *Dinetah* of their current Skinwalker scourge. At least, not for long.

So, why had the Skinwalker ghost appeared to her? Dammit. He needed some advice here. Things weren't making sense. This seemed to be a problem beyond his capabilities to solve alone, which didn't happen too often. Maybe he was too close to the subject. But he knew where he could go to get help.

Returning to the kitchen, he retrieved his cell phone. Michael felt grateful for being part of the Brotherhood, as he had innumerable times in the past. They were always ready with advice and help. And man, did he need them this time.

Lexie rolled over and found sunlight streaming through the window. Jack? She sat straight up in bed and had a meltdown. It wasn't until she had jumped out of bed and looked around that she remembered the reason Jack hadn't awoken her at his usual early hour. She was in Michael's spare bedroom, and Jack was spending the night with his Navajo relatives. He was fine.

Collapsing back on the side of the bed, she tried to catch her breath and quiet her nerves. For the first time in four years, someone else was taking care of Jack's needs. She had to be able to handle it.

As her breathing and heart rate dropped back to normal, Lexie began hearing voices. But they weren't from any spirits this time, and they seemed to be coming from someplace else in the house. At first she thought it must be a TV, or maybe it was Michael on the phone. The longer she listened, the more she thought not. Someone besides Michael was definitely in the house.

Curiosity drove her off the bed and had her slipping into her jeans and T-shirt. She dug for her watch in the bottom of the waterproof backpack Michael had rescued from the trunk of her car. Seven o'clock. Wasn't it awfully early for visitors?

What if it had something to do with Jack?

At that scary thought, she didn't bother with brushing her teeth or putting on shoes. Combing her fingers through her bed head hair as she went, Lexie raced toward Michael's kitchen. Clearly hearing his familiar voice by the time she reached the doorway, she skidded to a stop and plastered on a calm face for his benefit.

"Good morning." The words came out as casually as she could make them sound while strolling into the kitchen.

"Ah, Lexie, here you are," Michael said. He gave her an odd look, no doubt wondering about her bare feet and sleep tossed looks. But then with an almost imperceptible shrug, he introduced her to the Navajo man beside him.

"Dr. Ben Wauneka is a clan cousin and an old friend," Michael said with a solemn face. "He runs a medical clinic on the rez. And he's also a well-respected Navajo medicine man."

"A medicine man—like you are?" Lexie was fascinated by Michael's friend.

Dr. Ben's long, walnut-brown hair was pulled back in a bun at the nape of his neck, and he had a blue sash tied around his forehead. He had the most penetrating eyes Lexie had ever seen.

"Yes," Michael answered. "Though his practice is slightly different than mine. Ben combines his with his medical practice and uses crystals to diagnose illness."

When Ben Wauneka turned a half smile in her direction, his amber eyes seemed to see right through her skin. Or maybe it was more that he'd found something inside her gaze no one else had ever spotted at first glance. Whatever it was, his steady stare made Lexie's throat tighten with nervous energy.

But Ben's look was definitely not doing anything to her in the same sensual, electric way Michael's gaze always affected her. No, his was more in the way of someone who has just found out all your carefully guarded secrets.

"Is Jack all right?" The question just popped out when Lexie couldn't stand not knowing if he'd brought bad news.

"Of course he is. Why wouldn't he be?" Michael asked easily as he took down three mugs and began to pour. "Let's sit and have coffee. Ben has a couple of questions he'd like to ask you."

When they were seated at the kitchen table, Lexie found she could barely contain her jittery nerves. Why was this physician-slash-medicine man here anyway? And what did he want with her?

Ben placed his hands around his mug and stared down at the steaming liquid for a second before beginning. "Michael has told me of your ghost visions. Would you mind answering a few questions about them?"

As Ben looked up at her, his eyes suddenly seemed so full of concern it finally made Lexie's body begin to relax. "No, I suppose I don't mind," she answered.

Ben pursed his lips, thought a moment, then began again. "I've read a little about psychic phenomenon in general. But most of what I know I learned in med school."

He looked embarrassed. "I suspect what we heard there was not the complete picture—nor without a lot of prejudice."

He shot Michael a sideways glance, then continued to talk to Lexie. "Those of us who practice the traditional Navajo Way are very familiar with prejudice. When there's prejudice involved, fear moves in where understanding should be. I've certainly known fear to throw shadows over people's beliefs. I try not to succumb to that sort of thing myself. I would rather try understanding."

After taking another sip of coffee, Ben continued, "Michael tells me your mother also saw ghosts. Could you explain what you know about her visions?"

Lexie shot her own quick glance at Michael. He was sipping coffee and only seemed quietly interested in what she would say. She wished she could tell what he was thinking. Too bad she didn't read minds.

Sipping her coffee, Lexie took a second to wonder why she wasn't more intimidated by these two formidable looking Navajo men. But she wasn't at all. Somehow she just knew they were sincerely interested in her welfare. Which was kind of amazing when she thought about it.

Lexie took a breath and decided she might as well truthfully answer whatever questions they asked. Why not?

"The term used for what my mother experienced, and now for what I do, too, is being a *medium*. Mediums can contact—or are contacted by—people's spirits from beyond the grave. Somehow these spirits manage to come back from the other side. And usually, they have messages to deliver or particular warnings to give."

Ben nodded and added a thought of his own. "The *Dine* have seers—people who can foresee the future. Is it something along those same lines?"

She shook her head. "There are other psychics, with different abilities from mine, who can see the future," she explained. "They have precognition. But that's not what my mother—and now, I—can do."

Michael banged down his cup and interrupted. "Hold on. You seem to know an awful lot about this stuff. I thought you told me you'd always hidden from your so-called *gifts,* that you didn't want to think about them."

A surge of self-righteous anger rushed through her veins. "I said I *put away* the visions. I didn't say I wasn't curious about them."

Ben frowned at Michael. "What else can you tell us about the visions?" he asked in a conciliatory tone.

"Well, I've read about scientists who are conducting experiments with mediums. Their thinking now seems to be that *all* actions, including thoughts and emotions, have a positive or negative energy. And such mental energy goes out into the atmosphere something like radio waves. Apparently, strong emotions don't just disappear when a person dies.

"And I'd guess the energy from those kind of emotions can be picked up by people who are particularly sensitive," she added. "Like me."

Michael cleared his throat. Ben took a long, thoughtful sip of coffee. Lexie didn't much care what they thought about her visions. She'd had them—and couldn't seem to keep them from coming anymore—regardless of what they believed.

Finally Ben carefully set his mug down and looked steadily into her eyes. "You're in a strange position here in *Dinetah*. On the one hand, you're an Anglo and apparently here on a temporary basis. Ordinarily I'd advise you to say nothing about the visions and to leave as soon as possible."

"But…"

Ben lifted his hand to indicate he understood her hesitation. "Yes, I know. The bigger consideration is your son. He is Navajo, of the Big Medicine Clan as I am, and will be staying to learn about the Way. That changes things for you."

"There's another consideration, too," she put in. "I was told by a spirit that I'll be given information your people will need. So I can help your nation. I don't know exactly what it will mean, but I believe it's true."

"And not knowing totally what's involved, you still want to help us? You aren't afraid?" Ben asked softly.

Heck, yes, she was scared to death. But she gulped back the lump in her throat and shook her head.

Ben smiled and turned to Michael. "My instincts tell me this woman is not being used by the evil ones, but we need to be sure. Are you willing to do whatever is necessary to help her?"

Michael gave him a sharp nod. "Will you tell her what's involved now, or should I?"

Ben turned his head back in Lexie's direction. "If

word gets out about your seeing ghosts, there will be those who believe you have evil allies. They'll fear you, and perhaps even the evil ones themselves will take notice. Both of those would be intolerable situations for you and your son. But there are a couple of things you could do that can help your situation."

Lexie wondered if she was about to step off a ledge and walk into thin air. Man, if she'd thought being a medium was weird, these Navajo beliefs were beyond her imagination. She surreptitiously glanced at Michael, who seemed to be holding his breath and waiting for her to make some kind of decision.

"You must learn our ways and legends as soon as possible," Ben began again.

She nodded at him. That part had already been decided in her mind. Eager to make things right, mostly for Jack's benefit, she also realized she desperately needed the support of her in-laws in order for the two of them to stay on the reservation for any length of time. Lexie had to find the best ways to cement her recent and tentative relationship with their new family. Learning their ways was obviously only the first step.

"But before anything else happens," Ben continued. "Michael will make you a medicine pouch. Wear the pouch in full view and wear it always. It'll show your acceptance of our ways."

"Okay."

"The next step to take is for you to have a ceremonial Sing done in your honor."

"A Sing?"

"A medicine man chant and ceremony, designed to bring you back into the natural order of things. I would assume even the right Sing won't be able to *cure* you of your gifts. But it should bring you into harmony with the good spirits. And when a ceremony is done well, the People will more readily accept you amongst them."

"Did you have time to act on my suggestion?" Michael interrupted to ask Ben.

"Yes, Cousin," Ben responded. "I checked the archives of the *Dine* Hataalii Association this morning. You were right."

Ben turned back to Lexie. "There are over fifty different ceremonials in our traditions and not all *hataaliis* can perform every one of them.

"What you will need is an obscure Sing, an ancient derivative of the Evil Way ceremony. But the branch best suited for your situation is only practiced these days by one old *hataalii, Hastiin* Dodge Todacheene."

"Okay. So let's call him up and ask him to give me the Sing," Lexie volunteered.

"I'm afraid things aren't so easy in *Dinetah*," Ben told her with a wry smile. "There are people who live without electricity and running water in several areas of the rez these days. Many more do not even have telephones.

"But I did speak to *Hastiin* Todacheene's grandson this morning," he added. "The grandson told me his grandfather has been living in one of the canyons up in Monument Valley—near Stagecoach Wash—with one of the old man's daughters. I was given directions for you to follow that will take you there."

"That's the area near the ancient pictograph caves that I've been wanting to take a look at," Michael said. "We'll go there as soon as we can prepare for the journey. Tomorrow."

Lexie felt a shiver roll down her spine as both Ben and Michael sat quietly watching her reactions. Everything they'd said seemed so outrageous and different from everything she had ever known.

Yet every time whatever they'd said had seemed too unbelievable to accept, she simply remembered her vision of the angry old Navajo who'd looked like a dog.

Nothing could hold a candle to that in the scary, weird department, she supposed. So she would just have to find a way to reconcile *her* strange beliefs with *their* strange beliefs.

And try not to make a fool of herself—or die—in the process.

Chapter 6

"Watch me, Uncle!" Jack straightened his back, tucked his knees under him and looked the same as any Navajo child who had been born to sit astride a horse.

"Good for you, Nephew." Just a few minutes ago Michael had become holder of the pony's reins, the stand-in for Jack's grandfather.

Michael stood as close to the moving animal as possible, keeping a tight grasp on the pony's bridle. But Jack wasn't in the least afraid, and seemed to be thrilled to be in the saddle.

The three of them, Jack and Michael and his sister's pony, were the only ones in the arena at this time. Michael's mother had taken Lexie and Naomi shopping in Gallup for a couple of hours to buy clothes and new supplies, replacing what Lexie had lost in the flood. Jack's grandfather had gone inside the house for a conference call with other chapter councilmen. And Naomi's kids had not yet come home from school.

Michael would've preferred that he and Lexie get an early start on finding the *hataalii* Todacheene. But it was mostly his fault they hadn't. He had taken too much time this morning locating the objects necessary for her *jish*, the protective medicine pouch made out of cow skin. He'd been overly careful about finding and putting together just the right ghost-herbs, flints and ashes as needed. Then he'd taken extra time saying the blessings that would give the pouch its proper meaning. He'd even slid in a stone fetish made in the form of an eagle, and hoped it would add to her protection.

When he was done with it, Lexie had dutifully pinned the pouch to her jeans' waistband. But afterward, she'd looked up at him and seemed so vulnerable and lost that he had suggested they drive by his sister's house to check on Jack before doing anything else.

The minute his mother caught sight of them as they pulled into the gravel driveway, she'd begun making the rest of their day's plans on her own.

"Am I doing it all right?" Jack asked, bringing him back to the moment.

"Don't hold the reins so tightly." Michael showed him how to thread the reins through his fingers. "See? More like this." It was the same way he'd been taught.

Jack set his mouth in concentration. And it suddenly occurred to Michael that this boy's face had hardened in the exact same determined expression as Daniel's had back when he'd first learned to ride.

Michael's thoughts went into the past nearly thirty years to the time when he had been trying to teach his little brother how to handle a horse. Daniel had eventually surpassed his teacher and had become a much better rider than Michael ever was. Daniel was a natural.

In fact, Daniel had been a natural at most of the things he'd ever attempted. Bronc riding, basketball and women were among the things he'd been best at.

Absently running a hand over the pony's silky flank, Michael got lost remembering the many times he and his younger brother had competed. And thinking of the many disappointments he'd faced as the eldest son being second best.

To Michael's everlasting chagrin, their father often consoled him by saying he should be proud of his own accomplishments, and that he should be satisfied with the gifts he'd been given instead of wanting what Daniel had. Jealousy was not the true Navajo Way of accepting the natural order of things.

But for a too-tall and broad-shouldered Navajo teenage boy like Michael had been, being the smartest kid in school didn't count for much. Not when every other boy he knew dreamed of being in the summer rodeo or to going to the state basketball championships. Like Daniel.

Michael had been the "good" kid. The bright one.

Daniel was the "champ" and the "charmer."

Fortunately, their maternal great-uncle had taken Michael under his wing and began his *hataalii* training early. That great honor had eventually given him back some of his self-worth. And later on, so had graduating from college with two degrees by the age of twenty.

Out of the blue, Jack's knee seemed to automatically nudge the pony, and the animal picked up its pace.

Michael was amazed at how the boy knew many of the right moves to get what he wanted from the pony without being told. Lexie's son rode fluidly, as though he and the pony were already perfectly attuned after one morning together.

Michael put a hand on Jack's back and felt the excitement running through his little body. Too bad Daniel wasn't alive to see how his son took to riding.

Lost again in time, Michael remembered how hard he had tried to convince his baby brother to come home, especially when Daniel had married. By then his parents had already given up hope of their younger son quitting his roaming and playing ways. For years they'd begged Daniel to come back into harmony, to come back to the *Dine.* He had laughed at their old-fashioned values and called them boring.

But on the occasion of Daniel's wedding, Michael felt he should give it one more try.

After all, a married man might be ready to change his mind and put down roots. A family might make a man want to reevaluate his heritage.

But Daniel hadn't wanted to listen. Refused to listen. He was too busy trying to make Michael jealous. And Michael had too easily fallen right back into that same old trap.

Oh, he could've cared less about Daniel's money and his exciting job with the oil drilling company. The clothes, the expensive Las Vegas suite, none of it meant a thing.

Michael hadn't coveted any of Daniel's success or possessions. By that time, he'd completed his medicine man training and knew the Way to balance. Michael hadn't considered anything Daniel possessed worth giving up his traditional values. That is…until he'd met Daniel's new bride.

The mere sight of Lexie had been enough to send Michael right back to his anguished teenage years. Right back into his old green haze of jealousy. With one look, Michael would have gladly killed his brother for just a chance to be with her.

Those nontraditional and unbalanced emotions had hit him so fast they'd scared him, driving him out of town in a hurry—even before the wedding reception took place.

Jack's high-pitched, childish laughter suddenly brought Michael back into the golden sunlight of the day and out of the misty reaches of his memory. He swallowed down the lump of guilt he'd been choking on and reminded himself it wasn't his fault Daniel's son had no father.

But he couldn't quite get past the guilt of still wanting his brother's wife. So he did what he had done all those years ago. He put his urges and desires aside, trying to bury them so deep that they could never again see the light.

Once more Michael Ayze did the smart thing—the good thing—and chose harmony over need and want.

Back in Michael's kitchen after her shopping excursion, Lexie wondered what seemed different. When they'd left his sister's house a while ago, Michael had told her it was too late to start out to find the old medicine man today. But being late didn't seem to be what was bothering him.

"Would you mind going over to the college with me this afternoon?" Michael asked as he put away a few frozen casseroles and the new dish towels his mother had sent over. "I have a laptop in my college office I'd like to take with me tomorrow when we head out to find the *hataalii*."

She shrugged a shoulder. "Okay. But I thought you were on leave from the college."

His hair was still damp from a recent shower and he smelled good. Like sage and sunshine. He had on a pair of khaki pants and a yellow T-shirt and looked better than any man had a right to look.

"I am. But I still maintain an office and stop in now and then to check on the department." He dropped one of the towels without noticing.

Lexie bent to pick it up. When she straightened and gave it to him, their eyes met. The electricity between them could've lit up an entire city. She'd felt strong vibrations coming from him before, and imagined they were simply the physical, needy kind. Quite normal for two attractive people. But today everything seemed to have changed.

Regardless of his mother's insistence on a marriage, and despite whatever the two of them might be feeling toward each other, a relationship between the traditional Navajo medicine man and the Anglo psychic medium would surely not be in the stars.

She knew it. And she was positive he knew it. Yet, now she couldn't help wondering what being in his arms would feel like. She would never act on that curiosity, however. So she shrugged and turned away.

Fifteen minutes later they were back in his huge red pickup truck and on their way to the college. Lexie had changed into the traditional Navajo long skirt and long-sleeved maroon blouse her mother-in-law had bought for her. She hoped no one at the college would mind when a blond Anglo showed up dressed in traditional clothes. The new things somehow felt very comfortable on her.

"What are you going to be using the laptop for?" she asked Michael in order to fill up the silence.

"I've been researching an old *Dine* legend and my notes are on the laptop. I was hoping—"

"What's the legend?" she interrupted to ask.

Michael drew in a deep breath, and then let it out. "It's the Skinwalker origin legend. The story of the Wolf Clan, the evildoers in Navajo life who are as old as the tribe."

"Will you tell me the legend?"

"I can give you the most popular version," he glanced over at her through the corner of his eye. "But I'll need to shorten it a lot."

Lexie folded her arms under her breasts and waited.

"First of all, do you know who Changing Woman was?"

"The mother of all Navajos. The first woman?"

"Yeah, that's right, more or less. Her son, Monster Slayer, teamed up with another, Born of Water, and the two young men went out into the world to kill monsters. They were preparing the land as the chosen place for the People to live and thrive. As the two men went around, they made the decision not to kill any monsters who served a valid purpose."

"What kind of monsters were those?"

Michael scowled, but kept his eyes on the road. "Give me a second to tell this story the right way. You need to learn not to interrupt a Navajo. Breaking in on someone's thoughts doesn't follow the tradition. Only a white man is so impatient."

Lexie scowled too, but pursed her lips and waited.

"An example of the kind of monster the two men decided to spare," Michael began again, "was the Monster Who Eats the Flesh of the Dead—today we call that one the buzzard. They also saved Monster Who Brings Old Age—to us it's now known as natural aging and death. Some others they saved were Cold Woman—who brings winter and the different seasons—Poverty Creature and Hunger Monster.

"We can complain and ask why save these creatures, but the original lengthy legend explains how intolerable life would be without them. For instance, just imagine a world with no death and only more and more people to fill up the land. Each monster they saved has a hidden side which would make the world an infinitely worse place without them."

"What does this have to do with the Skinwalker legend?" The question slipped out before she could stop it.

Michael narrowed his eyes, but made no further comments about her big mouth. "Some of the really bad monsters hid and escaped being slain. The worst one of those got away by hiding in a deep cave under a large body of water.

"That particular monster was called Greed, the antithesis of the Navajo Way. Sometime later, Diving Heron dove into the water and secretly brought back Greed, in the form of the first medicine man. But Greed was shunned by the People. So he taught himself to change into the form of a wolf with extraordinary powers enabling him to walk amongst them and cause trouble. And thus he became the first Skinwalker."

"Cool story. But what exactly are you studying about it?"

"Lexie…"

"Sorry. Sorry. Tell it your own way."

"Another part of the legend says the first Skinwalker wrote his secrets down on special parchments and hid them in a cavern under a cliff that was reachable only by water. One of those secrets was supposedly the secret of longevity—or how to live forever."

"No kidding?"

When Michael's lips thinned and his eyebrows came together at her outburst, she clamped a hand over her mouth and suppressed a chuckle.

"Most wise men down through the ages have come to the conclusion that, unlike the Skinwalker story," Michael continued soberly, "the parchment legend probably had no basis in fact. In other words, it was just a good treasure story. But more recently, there have been findings suggesting otherwise."

She turned to him, fascinated. But bit her tongue rather than ask all the questions twisting in her mind.

When Michael remained silent for a long moment, she couldn't stand it anymore. "Are you going to look for the parchments yourself?"

This time, he didn't argue but simply answered her question. "After studying many of the obscure legends that have been handed down, I believe the *ancient ones* may actually have left petroglyphs with special warnings for the People. And I'm hoping they also left directions for finding those parchments. I have in mind looking for a few remote spots where the ancient drawings may be located."

Lexie hoped she'd finally learned the lesson of what Michael had said was expected in Navajoland. About not making a comment or asking a question until after the storyteller had a chance to add a last thought or fact. She stayed quiet, thinking of the many things she wanted to ask.

But after a few minutes of silence, Michael pulled his truck into the parking lot of the *Dine* College and parked next to the building marked Natural Science Lab.

"Come with me," he said, effectively dropping the entire discussion. "I hope this won't take long, but I don't want you sitting out here alone."

By the time she'd undone her seat belt, Michael had come around the truck, had her door open and was standing beside her with his hand held out to help her down. Unhappy about not getting her questions answered, she was still enthralled by his polite behavior. His brother had never been so thoughtful, that was for sure.

Taking Michael's hand, she slid out of the truck but nearly stumbled, and was forced to stop and rearrange the folds of her skirt. She wasn't used to wearing such a lot of material.

Michael waited until she'd straightened up again. Then he started down the walkway ahead of her.

She hurried to catch up. "Is your office in the Natural Science Lab?"

He shook his head. "I want to check on a colleague before we head over to the Behavioral Sciences building."

They made their way through the wide halls. Before long Michael stopped in front of a corner office door and knocked. No answer.

"Maybe your friend has gone home for the day," she suggested.

"Not likely." He knocked again.

Lexie heard someone calling out Michael's name. Glancing around, she saw a pretty young woman hurrying toward them down the hallway.

"Professor Ayze! Michael. It's great to see you." She had clear, bronze-colored skin and shiny black hair reaching all the way to her waist. She ran up to Michael, threw her arms as far as they would reach around his rib cage and pressed herself against his chest.

Lexie thought she was beautiful. But that thought brought with it an unwanted wedge of jealousy. She tried to tamp down on the green-eyed monster because, after all, she had no claim on him.

Michael leaned away from the woman's embrace but smiled at her. "Amber, I'd like to introduce my sister-in-law Alexis Ayze. Lexie, this is Assistant Professor of Botany, Amber Billie."

"Nice to meet you," Lexie murmured.

"Hi," Amber said with a beaming smile as she unlocked the office door. "Come in. I was just down feeding quarters into the junk food machines. But I think there's an old pot of coffee still on. Can I offer you any?"

Michael took the lead. "No, thanks. We can't stay long."

Lexie finally noticed the woman had been carrying a fistful of candy bars. The smell of chocolate nearly knocked her over.

"Well, how about sharing dinner with me then?" Amber held out an unwrapped bar containing peanuts and chocolate. "Anything with chocolate qualifies as a decent meal in my book," she said with a toss of her head.

Michael chuckled, but both he and Lexie politely refused the offer.

Amber leaned her bottom against a wide desk and smiled up at Michael again. Her eyes were ebony colored and on the smallish side, and Lexie amused herself by deciding the young woman had snake eyes.

"There's a couple of reasons why I came by," Michael told Amber. "First off, I wondered if you'd had a chance to contact the New Plant Tender."

"Dr. Wauneka? Sure did. I called her like you said. We traded information on plant species. She knew the exact location of where I could find *Erythrina flabelliformis* in bloom this late in the year."

Lexie laid a hand on Michael's arm to interrupt. "Dr. Wauneka is a she?"

Michael threw her another scowl and Lexie backed up a step. Darn. She'd done it again. Opened her mouth and inserted her foot.

"*She* is Mrs. Dr. Wauneka," Michael told her sternly. "Ben's wife, Tory, who also happens to be a medical doctor."

"Oh."

Michael took advantage of Lexie having backed up. He turned his shoulder to talk to Amber and effectively blocked out Lexie and all her questions.

Ah well. She *would* learn the lesson of how not to interrupt with questions. Honestly she would.

Michael went on to talk to Amber about some potion

he'd made up especially for her. Lexie didn't catch the entire drift of the conversation. But at one point she did overhear something about an owl who was apparently giving the assistant professor problems.

Lexie thought that was rather odd. How could an owl cause big trouble? Then again, maybe it had been hooting at her window all night.

In a few minutes they bid Amber goodbye and were on their way toward the Social and Behavioral Science building. It couldn't have been too soon to suit Lexie.

As they were about to enter through the side door, however, a skinny middle-aged man came bustling out and nearly ran right into Michael.

"Ah, excuse me." The absentminded looking guy had a scraggly ponytail, was tall and extremely thin. As tall as he was, though, he had to look up to see Michael through thick-lensed glasses.

"Quite all right, Richard," Michael said with a smile. "No harm done."

"Michael. I thought you were on leave. What are you doing here?" The man peered over the rim of his glasses toward Lexie. "And just look. Here is the very Anglo woman we've been hearing so much about."

Lexie could feel Michael stiffen beside her. "Dr. Yellow Horse, this is my sister-in-law Alexis Ayze. What exactly have you been hearing?"

"My, my. I'd imagined the reason you'd come to the campus was because you'd heard the stories," the other man said in a conspiratorial whisper.

He turned his head and looked all around like he wanted to be sure he would not be overheard. "You know that young Professor Gorman? He's a big lug of a guy—even bigger than you. Teaches beginning psych?

"Well, he's organized an anti-Skinwalker group while you've been gone. Managed to recruit a couple of the newer professors and quite a few students, too."

Lexie watched Michael take in the information without making a comment. But she could tell he was carefully processing everything he heard.

"What does any of this have to do with my sister-in-law?" he asked after a moment.

"I've only heard rumors, mind you," Dr. Yellow Horse said. "And I have no wish to sanction such superstitious ideas myself. But I do understand that this Professor Gory—oh, that's the name some of Gorman's students have given him—" Dr. Yellow Horse interrupted himself "—anyway, supposedly he has accused you of…uh…conspiring with witches."

"I see," Michael said in such a low tone he could scarcely be heard two feet away.

"Oh, yes. He claims you've abandoned your traditional medicine man training and are holding unexplained chants and strange ceremonies—even taking the unusual step of making your parents leave their own home."

Like Michael, Richard Yellow Horse lowered his voice to a near whisper after throwing a sideways glance toward Lexie. "Professor Gory also claims you've brought an Anglo witch onto the rez to help you with your evil deeds. And now the two of you are living together, without the benefit of a traditional marriage."

Michael glared at the other man. "I wouldn't pass along wild rumors if I were you, Richard. You never know who might be listening."

"Right. Of course, I won't say anything. I've known you since I started teaching here ten years ago. I would never for a moment doubt your traditional beliefs."

Michael stood silently and stared at him. The quiet scrutiny was making Lexie uncomfortable, and it seemed to do the same for the other professor as well.

"Uh," Dr. Yellow Horse finally hedged uneasily. "If you didn't come to have it out with Gory and his group, why are you here? Are you coming back to work?"

"I came to pick up my laptop."

"So are you going to begin again with your research? Working on the same legend as before?"

"Yes. I've had several new ideas of where to look for the pictographs. I'm certain I'm getting closer to an answer."

"How thrilling. I'd be happy to offer my assistance. You know you can always call on me."

Michael nodded and thanked him stiffly for the offer. Then he took Lexie by the elbow and stalked off to his office.

Not more than twenty minutes later, Michael found himself grinding his pickup's transmission into second as he pulled out of the college parking lot and onto the highway with a squeal of tires. He hadn't uttered a single word in that whole time, but he was still seething inside.

Lexie hadn't said anything, either. He wondered if she was upset, or maybe scared.

"You okay?" he asked as he drove the truck around one of the detour barriers and down onto a gravel side road. Would the Navajo Nation never finish their incessant road projects?

She nodded without a word.

"You did an excellent job of remaining still back there, by the way," he told her softly. "On the other hand, Richard only made a fool of himself by repeating such trash. You've learned your first lesson in living the Navajo Way. Wait and listen. Richard should relearn the lesson himself."

"You're not upset by the rumors he told?" she asked.

"Not at all. Are you?"

She shrugged. "It's not my place. I can certainly move out of your house if it turns out I'm causing you any trouble, though."

That was exactly what had made him so angry. He'd known those damned rumors would worry her unnecessarily.

"You don't..." He had to pause and clear his throat, deciding to explain in a different way. "I'd already been informed about that anti-Skinwalker group a few weeks ago. I'm not worried about what they have to say. To traditionalists, anyone who would form a public group to talk about witchcraft is probably a witch themselves. Talking about Skinwalkers in public is taboo."

"Do you think that Gory professor is really a Skinwalker?"

"Maybe." It actually was a possibility that he was. But then again, the idea seemed too obvious.

"Oh..." Lexie jumped, touching the medicine pouch pinned to her skirt. "Something's wrong. The pouch is getting warm—it's almost too hot to touch!"

He had hoped the eagle fetish would warn her of trouble if she was in any danger. But what was the trouble now?

Michael glanced in his rearview mirror and caught a glimpse of a dusty gray pickup following them. Its windows had been darkened and the driver seemed to be hanging back for no reason.

Tapping the brakes lightly, Michael slowed his pickup to a crawl. The other driver did the same, keeping the exact distance between them.

Saying Navajo curses under his breath, Michael stood on the gas. He didn't have a clue what this guy was up to, but he had no intention of taking any chances with Lexie.

Chapter 7

Michael shot a glance at Lexie. Her eyes were wide as she hung on to the passenger door handle with a death grip. But at least she didn't look hysterical.

Drooping shadows of dusk cloaked the view out the back window. Michael gritted his teeth when he realized the next few yards would bring them onto a dirt road near the mountain village of Tsaile.

He flipped on his headlights, more to warn people they were coming than for seeing ahead, and slowed down. As he had known it would, when they hit the combination dirt and gravel, spray flew up on both sides of the truck and rooster-tailed behind them, blocking out what was left of the light filtering down through the trees.

Except for straight ahead, Michael couldn't see a thing. Where had the gray truck gone?

Murmuring a chant under his breath, he took the first turn away from the houses and hogans and onto a twisting canyon drive. He knew these mountain roads. He'd driven them ever since he'd been a boy of eleven and his father had given in and said he was tall enough to learn to drive.

Here on the western slope of the Chuska Mountains, forests of tall ponderosa pines, piñon and juniper grew right up against craggy peaks. Those same evergreen trees were also found at the bottoms of steep canyons, and had even managed to flourish around the two-ton boulders that stuck up out of the ground as though some giant had pitched them there like baseballs.

"Where are we going?" Lexie sat with a stiff back, staring out at trees that seemed to be closing their ranks around them. Sheer cliffs peeked through each small clearing as the truck flew by.

"We've got company," Michael said with a gesture to the road behind them. "I'm trying to maneuver him to come close enough so I can figure out who he is."

"Company? Why don't you just pull over and say hi?"

Michael was actually amazed to find he had the wherewithal to chuckle and drive *and* keep an eye on the clouded back window all at the same time. But staying within the moment and not being caught up with a beautiful woman like Lexie was what he needed to focus on right now.

"I'm concerned his intention is to hurt us," he managed, while holding in the smile. "He keeps hanging back, but staying too close for comfort—"

Michael's words were suddenly interrupted by a crashing thud just as their pickup lurched ahead. The damned bastard in the gray pickup must've rammed them from behind.

Michael was forced to react fast, trying to keep his truck on the road. Finding himself grasping the steering wheel as if the thing would buck out of his hands, he recalled the times he'd been gentling a horse.

"Oh. My. God." Lexie's face was pale and she seemed to be in full panic mode.

"Keep breathing and hang on," he advised as he fought to straighten the truck's wheels and gain control again. "I've got an idea."

Watching carefully, he stepped on the gas and raced down the winding road. In a few seconds Michael saw the spot he'd been waiting for. It was a sort of cul-de-sac lane, running off through the boulders and trees that had once been used by medicine men for a holy place of prayer.

He said his own prayers as he came to the turnoff. Driving as fast as he dared, he waited until the last possible second, stepped on the brake and dragged the wheel hard to the right.

His pickup made the turn on two wheels, spraying dirt, rocks and pine needles everywhere. He hoped the gray pickup was following close enough on their back bumper to miss the turn altogether. But not close enough to crash into them.

When his truck finally righted itself, Michael once again braked and managed to make the next curve at the end of the cul-de-sac on all four wheels. Another minute or two and they would be approaching the same road they'd just left. Michael flipped off his headlights and prayed there would be enough daylight left to see where he was going.

Almost to the place where the path met the dirt road, and through the growing shadows, he caught a glimpse of the spot he'd remembered. There were four building-sized boulders lining the road on both sides. Michael downshifted and jerked the wheel, driving his pickup off the path. He managed to dodge through the pines, coming to a stop directly behind the largest boulder.

Rolling down his window and snapping off the engine, he held his breath. Where was the gray pickup now? Had it made the turn? Would it drive right past them on the dirt road?

Turning to check on Lexie, he had to fight yet another smile as he found her holding her breath, too. Her eyes were shut and her fingers were white from grasping the door bar.

He reached out and gently squeezed her shoulder to give her strength. But he didn't say a word as he silently listened for the sound of an engine.

Lexie's heart was beating so erratically she was afraid it would jump right out of her chest. Why had they been chased and what would happen to them now?

As her heart rate slowed, she realized there was no noise—not even the sound of her own breathing. She chanced a breath and at the same time pried open her eyes.

It was dark enough by now that she could barely make out shapes through the front window. What was that straight ahead? A great big rock?

"Holy—"

"Shush." Michael put his fingers to her lips to keep her quiet.

They sat still for what seemed like eternity. Finally

the sound of an engine came through the eerie silence. But the noise seemed to be moving away from them.

Michael drew in a deep breath. "Guess they're giving up and leaving."

"I thought you wanted to find out who was driving. Why don't we go after them?"

He shifted in his seat and smiled at her. "I was curious at first—until things turned dangerous. I won't take any chances with you, Lexie."

Inordinately pleased by what he said, she couldn't remember ever feeling so cared for and special. Why did he have to do things like that? It was only going to make her life miserable in the end.

Michael turned on the engine and headlights and eased the truck out between the trees. "I'll find a way of learning who was driving the gray pickup without endangering our lives. I have a feeling it was someone from the college who'd been following us since we left the campus."

"Really? You mean a student?"

"Maybe," he hedged as he pulled out on the dirt road. "But why—"

"Fear is a great motivator," he interrupted. "People will do all sorts of strange things when they're afraid."

"Afraid of us? But why?" Lexie repeated herself as she shifted uncomfortably in her seat, trying to make sense of what he was saying.

He turned to her and his eyes went cloudy, betraying nothing. "In normal times there's a high degree of paranoia in *Dinetah,* Lexie. Traditional *Dine* live with many realities, and evil is something that's in their face daily. It surrounds them all the time. These days it haunts them even worse. Times are anything but normal in the Four-Corners."

"Are you talking about the new Skinwalker cult you mentioned before?"

He nodded and turned back to watch the road.

"So things are worse than usual with these Skinwalker guys," she muttered mostly to herself. "And this group at the college thinks we're part of the cult. And now one or more of them was following us trying to—do what?"

"I'd guess to warn us away."

She couldn't help what came flying out of her mouth next. "If things are this bad on the reservation, can't a bunch of you Navajos get together to fight off the bad guys for real? I mean, it would be better than letting some screwball college group threaten innocent people."

Michael kept driving and stayed silent for a long few minutes. Long enough for Lexie to worry she'd overstepped her bounds again.

Finally, he cleared his throat to answer. "That's certainly something to consider."

He'd come up with a pretty good nonanswer, she thought. Almost as good as Jack's when he knew he was in trouble.

But then what did she know of how best to take care of *Dine* witches? With every new revelation, she felt more and more as if she didn't belong here with these people and had better learn to keep her big nose out of their business.

Lexie decided to get ready for bed early. Michael had fixed them a light supper. Then he'd told her he had work to do, but they should be up and on the road by dawn.

She'd packed a few things just as he'd said to do, and they'd already loaded the back of the pickup with a bunch of their gear. Now while flipping off the last of the lights in the family room, she glanced around and smiled, noticing the color palette he'd used to decorate his home ran to the hues of nature, exactly like the clothes he wore.

There were rich browns, matching his eyes. Muted sage greens that brought the outside in. He'd even used touches of sunshine yellow and deep burnt orange like the cliffs she'd seen through the trees today.

He must be a man truly comfortable with nature.

Turning, she also couldn't help but admire his leather couches and the big masculine chairs. They seemed so much like him. A vision came to mind of his broad shoulders, tapering down to those narrow hips and muscular thighs...

Lexie caught herself before she went too far in that direction, shook her head at the foolish wanderings of her mind and snapped off the last of the lights. There was already a good chance, what with the excitement of the afternoon, she wouldn't be able to sleep. The last thing she needed tonight was a shot of erotic hormones fizzing through her veins.

Within a few minutes, her teeth were brushed and the clock set. She climbed between the sheets and closed her eyes, hoping it would not be a long night of tossing and turning.

"Wake up, Daughter."

Lexie blinked open her eyes with a start. "Huh?"

Twisting in bed to better see the clock, she was amazed the hands were reading four-thirty. In the morning? She must've dropped off last night like she'd been drugged.

The alarm wasn't set to go off until five-thirty. So what had awoken her now?

"I need a word, my daughter."

Sitting straight up in bed, Lexie let her eyes get used to the low moonlight coming through windows covered only by gauzy curtains. That is, she did until her vision cleared and she found a pleasant looking middle-aged Navajo woman sitting at the edge of her bed.

Whoa. "Who are you? And where'd you come from?"

Lexie pulled the blanket up under her chin and stared at the odd woman. Her first thought was that this person might be some nut from the college. Was she dangerous?

"Calm your fears. I am your son's paternal great-grandmother. I bring you no evil."

Oh right. Another frigging ghost.

Her nightmare visions were getting to be way too much. Enough with the ghosts, please.

Sighing in resignation, Lexie got herself together and decided to go along for now. "Did you say you were my son's great-grandmother? You look awfully young. How old were you when you…uh…died?"

"My time in this dimension was finished on the day my first grandson came into the world of the *Dine*."

"First grandson…Michael? You were Michael's grandmother, but you died the day he was born?"

Okay, now it was making a little sense. The woman was dressed in the long skirt and long-sleeved blouse outfit most traditional women still wore today. But her shiny ebony hair with no trace of gray was done up in two elaborate knots on the sides of her head. Very old-fashioned looking. She must've died young.

"Um, what do you want?" Lexie felt no fear at all. Still, this *was* a ghost sitting beside her.

The vision of the older woman smiled and Lexie began to relax a bit. "You have done well to bring my great-grandson to his home. The spirits of the ancient ones watch over him. He is destined to grow tall and strong."

Lexie let herself beam back, pleased by the nice image the older woman had painted. "Great, but—"

"Yet, his future is not assured," the woman broke in without letting her finish. "The future of all the children of *Dinetah* hangs suspended between good and evil."

"Are you talking about the Skinwalkers?" Lexie had interrupted and knew it wasn't right, but she didn't much care for this new twist.

The ghost frowned and put a finger to her lips. "I have a message. It is for you to help my grandson."

"For Michael? Well, I'll be happy to deliver the message, but I can't guarantee he'll listen. He doesn't want to hear from ghosts."

As the spirit reached out and took her hand, Lexie thought it should feel weird, holding hands with a ghost. But she just felt warmth and comfort.

"Using his good *Dine* character, my grandson knows the true Way. He is a great warrior who joins with other fine *Dine* warriors to vanquish the enemy."

Now that remark really did bring up some questions in Lexie's mind. Professor Michael Ayze as a warrior? She wanted to ask about it, but fortunately this time she remembered what she'd been taught and bit her tongue to remain still.

"Yet my grandson has been floundering recently. He lets distractions deter him from his destiny."

Did she say *distractions?* "Am I the one getting in his way?" All Lexie's lessons suddenly went right out the window. "Are you saying I'm distracting him from some mission?"

The ghost patted her hand. "You will be both his greatest difficulty and his greatest joy, daughter.

"But you must fulfill your own destiny," the ghostly presence continued. "It will be up to you to bring our messages. You will be known as the Message Bearer. Throughout the ages, in times of greatest peril, there have been those who brought missives from great distances to the leaders of the war council. This role is to be a part of your destiny."

She had a destiny? Apparently so. "If being the Message Bearer is only a part of my destiny, then what's the rest?"

Smiling again, the ghost placed a gentle touch against Lexie's chest. "You will know that when your head accepts what is already here in your heart.

"For now, you must keep my grandson on the right path. He strays when he does not accept the warnings and messages of the ancient ones. Letting his head rule his spirit, he does battle with the wrong enemy."

Oh, man. Why did this message seem so confusing? Lexie had to hope all the messages wouldn't turn out this same obtuse way. If she was destined to keep seeing ghosts, she needed to be able to decipher what they wanted.

She began to feel growing sympathy with Michael for losing his head, because her own head was beginning to pound.

Closing her eyes and taking a deep breath, Lexie tried to gather her wits in order to ask the right questions. She wasn't sure why, but suddenly it seemed very important that she understand everything.

When she finally opened her eyes, the ghost of Michael's grandmother had gone and she was all alone.

A half hour later Lexie stepped out of the shower and toweled off. Her feverish mind churned in circles, desperately trying to put the things she'd learned together and make some sense of them.

Let's see. She got the part about being the Message Bearer okay. That was pretty obvious. The ghosts came, gave her messages and she turned them over to Michael. Sounded easy enough if she could only make him listen. And it would be something she could do to help the *Dine*.

Except… She had a gut feeling it wouldn't be wise to tell Michael about the message she'd just received— not just yet. For sure he would be unhappy knowing a ghost had been in his house. Even if it *had* been his own grandmother's ghost.

Sighing and shoving aside the tiny spurt of guilt about not sharing everything with Michael, Lexie stepped into her underwear and went to the closet to find something to wear for today. Absently, Lexie let her mind sort through the various things the grandmother ghost had said while she sorted through her meager clothing choices. If she couldn't talk to Michael about his grandmother's message, then she would have to figure it out all on her own.

Dine warriors. Those were the first words that had struck her as odd. *Warriors.* For real? Like an army?

Something else the grandmother had said seemed off. What was it again? Oh yeah, *war council.* Warriors and a war council. Was there a war going on she hadn't heard about?

Now wasn't that just a scary thought. A war occasionally caused civilian casualties. Chills ran down the back of her neck when she thought about Jack and the rest of the children getting caught in the middle of a war.

But Jack's great-grandmother hadn't seemed worried over the children's lives. Her major concern had been more about their futures in a dark world.

Well, Lexie guessed she would have to give in and ask Michael about the war. Such a huge thing was too important to skip. She'd find a way to ease into it, trying not to upset him too much.

Looking down at what she'd been doing, Lexie realized she'd dressed herself in jeans, a T-shirt and a flannel overshirt. Hmm. Yeah, the outfit should be fine for trekking out in the desert looking for an old wise man and caves with ancient writings.

Okay, good start. Now, should she wear old running shoes or brand-new hiking boots? Boots.

Boots? Shoot. She'd totally screwed up and packed her new boots in the truck last night.

She glanced at the clock which said it was almost five-thirty. Michael would want to leave in another twenty minutes or so.

Oh, hell. She'd wanted to be ready on time, and that would no doubt include wearing her boots.

Jamming her feet into the slip-on moccasins Naomi

had given her, Lexie decided Michael would never notice if she dashed out to the truck for a minute. He'd said not to leave the house during the night, but she would only be outside long enough to get her boots and it was almost morning.

She crept out the kitchen door and waited until her eyes grew accustomed to the dark. Earlier the stars and the half-moon had lit up everything outside her window. But now the vague beginnings of a cloudy gray dawn blocked out almost everything else in the sky. She could see well enough to walk to the pickup, but just barely.

As she tiptoed toward it, Lexie heard a rustling noise coming from the far side of the house. Was there some kind of animal out here with her? Uh-oh.

Running full out, she got to the truck in seconds, found her boots and then stopped, keeping still to listen for the noises. She held her breath and clearly heard it again.

Don't panic. If the sounds were coming from some nocturnal creature, whatever it was probably would be as scared of her as she was of it.

However, using caution was a lot smarter than being unprepared. Lexie bent and picked up a couple of the heaviest rocks from the side of the gravel driveway. Keeping a golf-ball-sized one in her hand, she stuck the other rock inside a boot, held both boots in the other hand and turned to run back to the house.

But just then she heard something sounding like— snorting. Pretty loud snorting, too, and with a muted growl tacked on at the end. It wasn't a noise that seemed like meowing or croaking or anything else that might mean it was coming from a critter who would be frightened of her.

Peering off into the darkness while tightening her grip on the rock, Lexie saw an outline of some large beast moving in a wide arc around the house, away from where she stood.

But the scary shadow wasn't the sight that made her gasp and freeze in place.

No. The sight that shocked her and left her holding her breath was the outline of Michael standing with his back to her as he faced the rising sun. And he was naked from the waist up. The crazy man didn't even have sense enough to wear a shirt, and the air this morning was nearly freezing.

She wondered what he could be doing as she watched him throw something like dark confetti into the air. Was he chanting? She'd already learned chanting meant prayers for the medicine men.

The idea that he might be praying forced her to turn away from the sight of those phenomenally broad shoulders and tight muscles, rippling with every movement. She blinked and averted her eyes, trying to forget the sensual image of the man she'd actually begun drooling over.

Wiping her mouth on her sleeve as she turned, she found herself facing the sight of the large creature. Only this time the thing was moving quietly through the brush in a direct line toward Michael. Was it going to attack?

The animal moved out of the shadows of a juniper and lumbered closer. Lexie saw the beast clearly for the first time as it stopped, stood still and sniffed the air.

A bear! Going for Michael?

Lexie never gave it one moment's thought. She took

off toward the bear at a dead run, screaming at the top of her lungs and winding up to throw the rock.

No chance, bear. Get away from him.

Chapter 8

Michael spun around when he heard the commotion behind him. What he saw nearly stopped his heart. Lexie was sprinting toward a bear.

He quickly realized this was no ordinary bear. A damned evil Skinwalker had dared to come close to his home. But what was his crazy Anglo sister-in-law doing?

The Skinwalker Bear would not be able to cross the Brotherhood boundary around his house that Michael had set down long ago with magic blessings. Unfortunately, Lexie didn't know what he'd done and was going to run right past the invisible line in her zeal to chase the Bear away.

He didn't have time at the moment to consider whatever would possess a lone woman to go up against a full grown bear, let alone a Skinwalker Bear. All he could think of for now was what he could do to keep her safe.

The Bear snarled and snapped his jaws as he stood up on his hind legs in a threatening stance. The otherworldly creature towered above Lexie at a height of over eight feet. Michael would never be able to stop her in time.

Closing his eyes, he began the ancient chants that would propel the Skinwalker into leaving. He hoped it would be enough to save her.

When he opened his eyes again, she'd stopped just short of the invisible boundary line and seemed to be in the process of throwing rocks at the evil one. Rocks? At a Skinwalker?

It would've made him laugh if it hadn't been such a deadly game. Michael continued singing every anti-Skinwalker chant he'd ever learned while he ran toward her.

The Bear ignored Lexie's attempts to make him leave and made angry swipes in the air as Michael came up behind her. With a deadly glare at Michael and one last ferocious roar, the evil monstrosity finally backed away from the invisible boundary and ducked into the piñon shadows.

But there was enough half-light for both of them to see the beast's image as it appeared to shrink down. Right before their eyes the Skinwalker turned back into a man.

Michael's chanting had worked. He quickly moved closer to Lexie, took her by the shoulders and held her steady—keeping her from stepping over the invisible line while he tried to make out the beast's human form. Who was this Skinwalker in real life?

But the man behind the Bear disappeared into deep brush before Michael could get a good look at him. Michael's greatest concern now had to be Lexie.

He twisted her around so he could study her expression. "Are you okay?"

Her face flushed while she opened and closed her mouth in an effort to speak. "Did you see...?" she sputtered. "That was... Wasn't it?"

"Lexie, talk to me. Are you hurt?"

She shook her head and continued. "I thought it was going to attack you. The horrible thing wasn't real—but it wasn't human either. Oh, I..." Tears welled in her eyes and she began to shake.

Michael couldn't stand seeing her like this, especially now the danger was over. "Come here," he said as he dragged her close and wrapped her in his embrace.

She fell against his chest and exploded into deep sobs that wracked her body with violent shivers. Her copious tears soaked them both.

"Go ahead," he whispered. "Let it out. But remember, you're safe with me. Nothing can harm you."

Since that hadn't been strictly true so far, Michael chided himself. He should've been paying closer attention. Protecting her was his job while she was in *Dinetah*. But he swore nothing *else* would get close enough to hurt her.

Her shaking began to subside after a few minutes. But the tiny, sad mewling noises she was making deep in her throat went on for a long time afterward. It was enough to break his heart.

He would have done anything to save her from the Skinwalker terror she'd had to face. And now he would be forced to explain every bit of the horrible situation the *Dine* currently faced in the Four-Corners. It wasn't something he was looking forward to.

Standing there and holding her close, Michael felt her feminine warmth spreading through his own chilled body. She inched closer and took hold of his biceps, apparently seeking more stability and comfort.

He'd give her anything she wanted. It hadn't escaped his attention that this extraordinary woman had torn out after a bear she'd thought was going to cause *him* harm. Like a tough little mama hen, protecting her chicks. What a woman. She was spectacular.

The atmosphere around them changed all of a sudden. Instead of wanting to offer her his strength, he began to feel her own tough spirit as it seeped into his body along with her warmth. And then…the idea of her strength began turning him on.

Just remembering how brave she'd been to face the terror made him want to experience some of her special strength in a more personal way.

He looked down at the top of her head as she snuggled into his chest, and he wanted her. No matter that any intimacy between them would be totally inappropriate.

It was all he could do not to touch her hair, not to lift her chin and dip in for a taste. He hadn't wanted anything so badly for as long as he could remember.

Trying to find somewhere else to look, or to somehow manage to close his eyes to the lust, Michael found he couldn't do anything at all. The two of them seemed to be lost in a kind of dreamworld as it spun out of control.

He couldn't move away from her warmth and need, and he couldn't get as close as he wanted without upsetting the tender balance of friendship and trust they'd managed to reach.

The clear blue morning sky and the green earth of late summer swirled around. Nothing else was in focus but her. Nothing but Lexie in his arms.

At last she wriggled against him and raised her head to look up into his eyes. "I'm sorry," she said in a faint, wispy voice. "I never fall apart like this. I'm usually much stronger. I don't know what got into me."

He shook his head but couldn't speak. He'd wanted to jump to her defense. She had every right to go a little nuts after everything she'd been through in the last few days. He thought she was the bravest, the strongest woman he had ever known.

But he couldn't get the words out.

For a supposedly smart guy, Michael did a really dumb thing then. He raised his hand and thumbed away the leftover tears from under her eyes. But her skin felt so soft under his fingertips that he got jumbled up in the sensory impressions. His hand refused to leave her face as he cupped her jaw and stared into her slightly confused eyes.

Never taking her gaze from his, Lexie placed her palms flat against his chest. The move seemed very much like she'd gotten dizzy and was trying to steady herself again. But the zinging and electrified sensations coming from the spots where she was touching his chest made *him* dizzy and had apparently fried his brain. His mind must be gone, because the next thing he did was beyond stupid.

Fanning his fingers, he let them skim her jaw and slide down her throat. She closed those hazel eyes that had gone all golden and gooey, and a dreamy smile of pleasure took the place of confusion on her face.

Oh, hell. That did it.

It was beyond his ability to stop. He bent, placed tender kisses against her eyelids. But that wasn't nearly enough for him, so he nibbled his way down her throat and to the tiny indentation at the base. He found the utmost satisfaction in exploring each inch of new, forbidden territory.

His every sense became heightened, filled to the limit. The silkiness of her skin pleased both his fingers and his tongue beyond all measure. The way she smelled—all clean and floral—intrigued and delighted his nose. He thought she possessed her own special musk, some fragrance he couldn't name but decided it was something he would never forget. For the first time in years, he simply gave in and allowed his nose and eyes and mouth to take in every pleasurable sensation.

She leaned against him with feminine rounded curves and he grew hard in response. His sharp angles fit perfectly together with her woman's body. Like they'd been made to be that way.

As her body seemed to dissolve further into his, a moaning noise came from deep within her throat. Again, Michael couldn't manage to help himself. He was apparently doomed to make the big mistakes.

Lifting his head, he brushed his mouth against hers. Tentatively. He had to keep reminding himself she was the vulnerable one here. But all he wanted, all he desperately craved, was to know what she really tasted like.

When at last she opened her heavy-lidded eyes again, it was to begin a slow, close-up inspection of his face. As if she needed some clue from him about what to do next. He wasn't sure what expression she'd hoped to find, but in the next instant she closed the small distance between their lips and kissed him back. Much less tentatively than he had kissed her.

There was a kind of wildness behind her kiss. Absolutely nothing about her felt tame or motherly as she pressed her body up and down against his. Her tongue searched out his tongue, tangled as she licked and nipped at his bottom lip. She kept on and on, getting him more and more aroused, until at last he growled and melded their mouths together in a hot and wild eruption of passion.

As if of its own accord, his hand came up and cradled her breast. Ah, he thought absently, another perfect fit. He stroked her through the many layers of clothes until her nipple peaked under his attentions.

His own body's savage responses to her attentions finally sunk in to his numb brain and shocked him. She had blindsided him with a raging hunger he had never before experienced.

Now with a sudden and mostly unwanted instant of clarity, he realized they had to stop. Or he would have them both undressed and be inside her before she took her next breath.

"Lexie," he groaned against her mouth. "We can't. I can't."

"Excuse me?" She pulled back and blinked her eyes.

The look on her face nearly changed his mind again. Her lips were rosy and full from kissing him. Her eyes still held a dewy look and were slightly unfocused. She looked like a woman who had been thoroughly kissed, and who wanted much more.

Well, hell. So did he. But it wasn't going to happen.

"We don't have time to play games," he said gruffly.

"Games?" Her eyes lost that dewy look with a blink. The sensual haze was soon replaced by an angry, shooting glare.

"We can't let anything intimate grow between us," he tried to explain. "It wouldn't be right and we both know it."

He'd said the words without as much conviction as he'd hoped. "I'm your brother-in-law, dammit. Your child's uncle," he nearly cried with frustration.

She cleared her throat. "Your mother seems to think we should get married. Something *intimate* would have to happen between us then, wouldn't it?"

"You know a wedding's not ever going to happen," he snapped out. "It's an old, old tradition having nothing to do with modern life. Nor anything to do with *Anglos,* for that matter. My mother was just grasping at any way to keep her grandson with her."

As he finished his little speech, he found he couldn't bear facing her. Lexie's hurt expression made his chest ache. Michael turned around and furrowed his fingers through his hair in frustration.

A strained silence developed between them. He couldn't stand not knowing what she was feeling or why she had become so quiet. Was she hurt by what he'd said? Or mad at him? He hadn't meant to hurt her. In fact, he'd been trying to protect her.

He swung around—but she'd already moved away. He spotted her marching across his yard toward the pickup.

"Lexie?"

"Get a move on, Brother-in-law. You're wasting the morning. We have places to go, and you have a lot of explaining to do."

Lexie squirmed under her seat belt and slackened the tension for the moment by holding it out away from her neck. The stupid thing didn't fit her right. Like most car belts, it hit her about chin level. Why couldn't auto makers do a better job of making their belts for women?

Probably because the car makers were men. She wasn't terribly thrilled with men in general at the moment.

A half an hour after they'd started out from Michael's house, and her mood was hardly any more pleasant than before they'd left. The damned man had actually kissed her, got her juices flowing, then cut her off at the knees. A month might not be enough time for her to get over her anger.

He'd certainly been right about one thing, though. A wedding for the two of them was *never* going to happen.

She'd already made one huge mistake with her first marriage. Dan had been a charming jerk. Michael was an *arrogant* jerk. Marrying him would only be compounding the error.

She folded her arms across her chest and captured the belt under her breast so she could hold it down out of her way. Michael was definitely not going to be her next husband, not for any reason. Not even to please his mother, whom Lexie had decided she really loved.

And it would be a hot day in the Antarctic before she ever let him so much as touch her again. No *intimacy* for you, Brother-in-law, she swore to herself. Not even if your warm brown eyes do start begging for a kiss. It is *not* going to happen. *I have learned my lesson.*

Lexie had come to another decision, too. Jack belonged here on the reservation. And until she was sure she didn't belong here, she intended to stay in *Dinetah* and fulfill her destiny as the ghost's Message Bearer. No matter what the message "receiver" had to say about it. She owed that much to the *Dine*, and to her in-laws. They were helping her in her time of need; it was the very minimum she could do for them in return.

But first she needed to understand exactly what was going on in *Dinetah*. And since Michael was handy, he'd just been elected to give her all the answers.

"Okay, Brother-in-law, time to come clean. I'm guessing the creature we saw was a Skinwalker. I want to know what the heck has been going on."

The minute the words were out of her mouth, Lexie had already figured it out. Yesterday she had been the one to say they needed to band together to fight off the Skinwalkers. But that was what had already been happening, wasn't it? The *war* the grandmother ghost had talked about must be a war with the Skinwalkers, raging on the reservation right this minute. And damned if Michael Ayze didn't know all about it.

"Yes, the Bear was a Skinwalker," Michael affirmed in a near whisper and without taking his eyes from the road ahead. "It changed over to human form in front of you because I was saying an ancient chant designed especially by our ancestors to weaken Skinwalkers. We found the chant, along with—"

"*We* who?" she interrupted. "You Navajos have some kind of secret army, don't you?"

He gave an almost imperceptible nod of his chin. "At times I wish we were more of an army than we really are."

Taking a long breath, he finally continued, "Some time ago one of my maternal aunts, known then as the Plant Tender, was the first to discover that a new Navajo Wolf had taken over the Skinwalker cult and was covertly building his own army. She gathered together a group of young medicine men, choosing for the most part those of us who belonged to her Big Medicine Clan for security purposes. Her original aim was just for us to recognize the threat."

"You're all related? How many of you are there?"

"At first it was only a handful of cousins. We called ourselves the Brotherhood. More recently, we have recruited others from different clans to join with us. As the threat of the evil ones grew, we had to grow in response."

The whole thing sounded like a comic book superheroes' story to Lexie. But the Bear this morning had been anything but funny.

"How many Skinwalkers are in their army?" she mumbled.

He shot her a sideways glance and shrugged a shoulder in response. "No telling. Too many."

"So who's winning the war?"

A dark look passed over Michael's eyes. "I believe the Brotherhood has caused the evil ones enough trouble to slow them down. A while back Ben Wauneka learned the Skinwalkers were recruiting teenagers into their cult, and we put a stop to it. Now we know better what to watch out for."

"What *do* you watch out for? How can you recognize the bad guys?"

Shaking his head slowly, Michael answered softly, "You can't recognize them unless they've already changed over. Otherwise, they look the same as everyone else."

"So anyone could be a Skinwalker? Even me?"

"Not you." He'd said it with a smile, but Lexie didn't think it was at all humorous.

"Have you called for help? Does the U.S. government know what's happening? What kind of weapons do you use?" Another thought, far more serious and ominous, occurred to Lexie before Michael could answer those questions. "Has anyone been killed?"

Michael remained silent for so long Lexie began wishing she could take back the questions altogether. She didn't want to hear the answers.

"The best ways to fight the Skinwalkers is with ancient chants and potions, not M-14s and rockets. Besides, the U.S. government would scarcely believe the reality of our war. You probably wouldn't have believed it either until you saw it with your own eyes."

Well, that part was true enough. But boy did she believe it now.

"The Skinwalkers usually attack covertly," Michael went on. "And they seldom use modern weapons. The Brotherhood has decided to keep the war quiet so as not to terrorize the *Dine* any more than necessary.

"So far," he continued with a heavy sigh, "we've only had one fatality in the Brotherhood. The Skinwalkers have *not* fared as well."

Lexie wasn't sure he would say any more. After a

moment, his eyes grew weary but he stayed focused on his driving. "My aunt, the Old Plant Tender, was killed trying to save a young woman during a skirmish with the Skinwalkers."

"I'm so sorry," Lexie cut in. She was mostly sorry she'd asked and didn't want to hear anything else.

He finished his thought. "That same young woman has now taken on the Plant Tender's responsibilities out of respect for her savior. And, she also happens to be married to my cousin, Ben."

Lexie was shaking her head in sympathy over the tragic death when she remembered already hearing about the New Plant Tender from the young woman assistant professor at the *Dine* College. What else had the assistant professor and Michael been talking about? Oh, yes, an owl.

"You told me once what kinds of animal forms these Skinwalkers can take, but I forget them now. I definitely remember the wolf from the Skinwalker origin legend. And I certainly saw the bear. What else was there?"

"Tradition surrounds which specific animal forms can be used by the evil ones. Throughout the years there have been stories of Skinwalkers who took the form of snakes, ravens and vultures, wild dogs—"

"How about an owl?"

Michael nodded again. "The Burrowing Owl is an ancient enemy of the *Dine*. The specific animal form that the evil ones choose depends on what kind of treachery that Skinwalker wants to cause."

Something else hit her then. "Oh, I remember you telling me about the wild dogs. Like the ghost I saw in your mother's house. Right?"

Michael screwed up his mouth as if he'd tasted something sour. "Enough questions for now. Why don't you practice becoming more like the People and keep quiet for a while. You wanted to learn the traditions for your son, didn't you? All your questions will be answered in time."

Of all the imbecilic, rude and arrogant jerks…

One of these days Michael Ayze would have to listen to *her* stories. She was suddenly determined to become the Message Bearer, despite what he thought about her visions and her questions.

Lexie sat back, thinking about ways to explain her vision of his grandmother and about the message she had been given. The man was forever talking about the Navajo legends and traditions, but he wasn't much of a listener.

She had a feeling he might be in for a big surprise. Wouldn't it be funny if she was the one who ended up having the very answer he needed the most?

Michael was having trouble concentrating on the road while Lexie sat in stony silence in the passenger seat. There seemed to be an eight-hundred-pound gorilla sitting in the front seat between them.

It was the damnable kiss. He'd thought and thought about what had ever possessed him to do such a thing. But thinking about the kiss so much was becoming problematic.

Because what he really wanted to do was kiss her again. He was having trouble thinking of anything else. Moving around uncomfortably in his seat, he became aware that another part of his body stood ready to take over for his brain and stop the thinking altogether.

Many years, a half a lifetime ago, was the last time

he'd made out in a truck. But the idea of throwing her into the narrow backseat and having his way with her was gaining a lot of ground in his clearly sex-crazed mind.

There were so many reasons why the two of them being together would be a bad idea that he could barely count them all. They were going to have to work as a team. He'd already promised his mother he would take care of Lexie and give her the job as his assistant. And now he needed to protect her from whatever Skinwalker evil came her way, too.

A temporary fling was the only kind of relationship he could ever have with Lexie. She hadn't been raised in *Dinetah* and would never be able to understand why he wanted to spend the rest of his life here. In a few weeks or maybe months, she would be ready to go back to her idea of civilization. It was bound to happen, despite her protests to the contrary.

This place was and always had been his destiny. It had taken him all those years of college and teaching whites to realize how much he belonged here. His one everlasting regret was that he couldn't have made his brother realize his destiny also lay in the Four-Corners.

Michael thought then of his brother's son. Would there be enough time for Jack to find his own destiny here? Maybe Lexie would consider leaving Jack behind with his grandparents when she left so he could truly learn the Way.

Whoa. Now his thinking was getting off into the ridiculous and fanciful. Considering a temporary fling with her was one thing, but the idea of Lexie leaving her child was totally out of line. No way would the mother hen ever walk away from her chick.

Enough. The air had suddenly turned stale inside the cab of his truck. He needed to get away from all this thinking and temptation for a moment.

As if he could...

Chapter 9

Michael pulled his truck into the large parking lot connecting the Black Creek Trading Post to a convenience store and takeout. He'd stopped at this place so he could get enough space for breathing room away from Lexie for a while.

"You going to wait in the car?" he asked, trying not to show the hope in his voice. "I'll only be a few minutes. I want to talk to a guy in the trading post."

She turned to glare at him and he felt the prick of her anger running down his neck and landing in his chest. He didn't want her coming with him. The trading post owner was a traditional Navajo and might have heard the rumors about Lexie from the kids at the college. Even though Lexie still wore the medicine pouch he'd made for her, not many people who believed in witches would want her around until she'd had the special Sing done.

"I'm hungry," she said with a sniff. "We missed breakfast. I'll go get something from the convenience store, if it's all the same to you."

He figured it should be okay for her to be seen in the convenience store. During the weekdays the newer stores in the area had mostly older whites or modern Christian Navajos working behind the counters.

"Fine," he said as he pulled a few dollars out of his pocket and handed them to her. "Here you go. Don't take too long."

"What's this for?"

"Food. They use actual United States currency here and that much should be enough for breakfast."

She stiffened her back and narrowed her eyes at him. "Not funny. Besides, I have a few dollars left. I don't need your charity."

Damned woman. "It's not charity. You are on my payroll as of this morning. Consider it a perk of the job. Or as an advance, if you're being stubborn."

Opening her door, Lexie swung her feet out but turned back for one last parting shot. "I choose the perk. Thanks, boss man." She flashed him a phony smile and climbed down from the pickup.

They went their separate directions. And he was never so glad to be out of someone's presence in his entire life.

As he stepped up to the trading post doors, though, he couldn't help shifting his gaze toward her. Would she really be okay by herself?

He saw her striding across the pavement with her chin held high and her hips swinging. It was a tantalizing view and he couldn't help taking a moment to admire what he thought of as one of the most spectacular sights around.

Unlike him, though, Lexie never hesitated for a moment or even bothered to turn as she dragged open the heavy glass doors and stormed into the store. Still angry. Maybe he ought to find a different way of dealing with her. What he'd been doing didn't seem to be working.

When Michael realized he'd been staring for over a minute at the empty spot where she'd last been, he mentally kicked himself and went inside. It was stuffy in the close air-conditioned interior of the old trading post. But the place smelled just the way he remembered from his childhood. A combination of herbs, coffee beans and peppermint candy. Every time he smelled any of those scents, he went right back to his beginnings.

This morning there wasn't one other person in the front of the store. For over a hundred years trading posts had been the local meeting spot for "sheep-camp" traditional Navajos, the one place where they'd buy or trade for supplies and catch up on the news. Today, quite a few of the old trading posts on the reservation had closed and stood abandoned in favor of the Navajo Nation's more modern grocery stores.

In fact, Michael didn't intend to buy anything, either. But he couldn't help feeling regret and nostalgia when he saw the untouched shelves of canned goods and while he watched dancing dust motes play in sunlight streaming through dirt-streaked windows. Low stacks of twenty-five-pound flour sacks, set out in the front of the store to entice customers, seemed almost to have petrified right where they sat. How sad.

"*Ya'at'eeh,* Professor *Hataalii.* It's been some weeks since we last saw you." The familiar voice shouted out to him from behind the rows of groceries.

Michael walked down the center aisle and found the owner of the voice, proprietor Nokai Joe, sitting on the very same old stool behind the very same old counter as always. The man had probably sat there in that same exact way every day for the last fifty years or so.

Hastiin Joe was much smarter than most trading post owners, though. He'd seen the tide changing several years ago and had moved his operation to the main highway. At the same time he'd added a convenience store, takeout and gas station. Now he did business with more tourists than *Dine.*

But obviously not here in the old-fashioned store. The place seemed utterly devoid of any business activities.

"*Ya'at'eeh,*" Michael answered in traditional greeting. "How are you feeling, my friend? Is the arthritis any better?"

"Yes, *hataalii.* The poultice you made for me a few months ago has freed me from the pain in my knees. Have you come in for payment?"

Traditional Navajos, especially the old ones, refused to use modern medicines. Most had never even taken an aspirin. Fortunately, the ancient medicines and chants usually worked just as well for them.

Michael surreptitiously studied *Hastiin* Joe, without blatantly staring in a non-Navajo manner. The salt-and-pepper hair had been a part of the trading post man's appearance for as long as he could remember. And the hair hadn't changed a bit. But the grooves in his forehead and the lines around his eyes seemed to have somehow miraculously lessened with time.

It caused Michael to wonder if Joe had found a hidden fountain of youth.

Except for wearing new glasses, the older man looked younger than ever. Michael wasn't particularly fond of his friend's new oval glasses. They were a surprising fashion statement on such a traditional Navajo, and made Joe look as if he was one of those young superintellectuals. Joe was smart in ways most people would never know, but he was no youthful genius.

"I have come to trade information for medicine," Michael finally answered. He knew Joe's interest would be piqued by haggling. It was what a trading post proprietor lived for.

The old man's eyes twinkled. "Sit down. I'll pour us a cup of coffee." This was the way of most normal social rituals for the Navajo. They had coffee over legends, stories, along with every transaction and event.

After Michael had perched himself on a tall stool next to Joe with coffee mugs in front of both of them, his old friend began trade negotiations for information. "What can I tell you that you do not already know, Professor?"

Michael reminded himself to go slow in the traditional Navajo manner. "How's business going in the trading post?"

"I am comfortable," Joe told him as he took a sip of the steaming liquid.

At Michael's skeptical look, the trading post man added, "You see the rugs on the wall behind me?"

Looking up at what must've been twenty-five

handwoven Navajo rugs on an overhead rack, Michael nodded.

"They are all sold and await shipment," Joe said with a wry smile. "If you'd like to bid on a rug just as beautiful as these, another group of equal value will replace them in a few days."

Those rugs were probably worth at least five thousand dollars a piece. Some, maybe double that.

"You must get lots of rich tourists coming through here," Michael said in amazement.

The older man sat, staring absently at a point on the wall, and let a familiar Navajo silence fill the air. Michael had been trained to be polite and outwait him.

At last, Joe spoke. "We trade now on the Internet. The Black Creek Weavers Association has their own Web site."

Michael knew there was no such thing as the Black Creek Weavers Association, but Joe had thoroughly surprised him. For many years, the proprietor had been taking rugs from the local women on consignment. Now, Michael would be willing to bet he was paying outright for the rugs—no doubt at about two thousand dollars a piece. And then reselling them on the Internet for huge profits.

Yes, indeed, Nokai Joe was one smart man.

"I think it is not my business information you've come to trade," Joe said with a covert smile from behind his coffee mug.

"You're right." Michael took a long slow drink of the coffee and let the silence drag on for a few more minutes. "I need information about a person we both know."

Joe began nodding and set down his mug. "There

have been rumors. This information will be useful for the witch woman you now protect?"

Michael was again surprised by his friend, but he recovered fast. "She is not a witch. But she has fallen across the path of evil. Dr. Wauneka has diagnosed her to be in need of a special Sing—one done these days only by the old *hataalii* Dodge Todacheene."

Joe's nodding stopped and he looked more thoughtful. "You are seeking *hataalii* Todacheene? He was in here buying supplies just last week."

"Here in Black Creek? Why? He's rumored to be living way over near Monument Valley with his daughter."

Michael had assumed the trading post man would have at least some information concerning the reclusive *hataalii.* Joe liked to trade in gossip almost as much as he liked trading in rugs. But Michael hadn't counted on Dodge Todacheene having left his daughter's hogan and then traveling all the way to Black Creek.

"The *hataalii* is an old man. Much older than me," Joe told him with a grin. "He says he travels on his last religious pilgrimage to the homelands and sacred places of his ancestors."

"But that could take months." Michael knew Lexie didn't have months to find her cure. "Did he say where he was going from here?"

"The old *hataalii* will first travel to his grandmother's birthplace in Tocito Wash. He wishes to begin at his beginning."

"Does he have relatives still living there?"

"I think so. But old man Todacheene intends to camp out under the stars like he did as a boy when he watched the sheep. Those are the kinds of supplies he acquired from me. Waterproof matches, plastic tarps. That kind of thing."

Michael figured the ancient *hataalii* must be nearly ninety. He also knew the old man was tough. But a man that age should have someone along to help him.

"What kind of car is he driving?"

"He drives the blue pickup he has owned for years."

"What? I remember his old blue pickup from when I was a boy. The thing must be thirty years old by now. I can't believe it still runs."

"It runs."

Michael stood, put his hands on his hips and made a decision. "The Tocito Wash area isn't too far from here. Just back up on the Western Slope of the Chuskas about an hour's drive. I guess we can take a detour to find the *hataalii*. If he's still around there."

Joe stood up, too, but didn't say anything.

"If we miss him and he happens to come back in here, will you tell him I'm looking for him?"

Hastiin Joe nodded silently.

Taking one of his college business cards out of his wallet, Michael handed it to Joe. "Here's my cell number. Can you call me if you see him? Or have *him* call me?"

"I will call."

Michael stepped back out into the parking lot and looked up at a cloudy sky looming over his head that was bringing a weepy, gray sadness to the day. He felt something evil suddenly creeping around and through the rocks, the plants and the very air he breathed. His skin crawled. It felt as if someone was watching him, and as though the whole world was holding its collective breath. Waiting.

Navajos had no word for *time* in their language. But

right now Michael was afraid that for Lexie, time was somehow running out.

Lexie sat back in her uncomfortable chair at the tiny table in the takeout place. The store had been swamped with customers a few minutes ago, but now everyone else had cleared out.

Taking another bite of her Navajo breakfast burrito, she couldn't get over how good it tasted. Scrambled eggs, beans, peppers and potatoes in a fry bread wrap. Yummy, but probably a thousand calories.

A stray thought ran through her mind. She'd much rather be tasting Michael's lips. Kissing him wouldn't add the pounds like this burrito would. However, being that close to him would probably be a lot more dangerous to her well-being than any high calorie food.

The very pregnant young Anglo girl who'd taken her money came out from behind the cash register to swipe at the table tops with a wet rag. "How's everything taste?"

With her mouth full, Lexie could only smile and nod.

"Been a busy morning," the girl supplied to fill up the gap. "You're not from around here. Where're you headed?"

The short, barrel-chested Navajo cook standing behind the grill looked up at her just then, and Lexie had the feeling he was paying close attention to whatever she would say. She forced a swallow in order to answer.

Before she could get a word out, though, both the girl and the cook froze and looked over her head as somebody came through the door behind her. Lexie turned, but she hadn't really needed to look. She knew who was standing there, just by the sudden electricity in the air.

"You ready to go?" Michael asked with a frown as he towered over her.

"In a minute. I'm not—"

"Now." Taking her elbow, he helped her from the chair.

"But I'm not done."

He picked up the waxed paper wrap containing the rest of her burrito and tossed it in a nearby trash can. "Bring the coffee. Let's go."

Furious, but too embarrassed to say anything in front of strangers, Lexie grabbed her coffee cup and went outside beside him.

By the time the air-conditioning had disappeared with the closing door behind them, she was winding up to really let him have it. "Just who do you…"

The rest of the words stuck in her throat as her plastic coffee cup dropped to the pavement, spewing coffee everywhere. There, in front of her eyes and painted in white on the side of Michael's red pickup, were the words Get Out Witch!

She was speechless. Was it meant for her?

"Sorry," Michael mumbled as he opened her door and helped her inside. "I should've warned you."

He slammed the passenger door behind her, picked up her now empty cup and pitched it into a barrel by the door and then climbed into the driver's seat.

"Buckle up," he urged in a low growl. "We're taking a detour into the mountains."

"But what do those words mean? Can you wash them off?"

He grimaced. "Apparently rumors are flying about

the white witch who's living with me. I didn't think the word would spread this fast."

Michael set his jaw. "Whatever they used for paint won't wash off. But we can cover it with dirt until I can get it painted over."

Shifting in his seat and hesitating with his hand on the ignition, he turned to fully face her. "Look, witchcraft and evil are a way of life out here. And right now, suspicions and rumors are running high. But any time someone is accused of being a witch or a Skinwalker, the People usually will grow to fear and despise them. Isolation is the worst thing to happen to a traditional Navajo, but that's what occurs in cases like this.

"It's something you need to consider again," Michael continued. "That, along with other things, like the danger from Skinwalker Bears for instance. Maybe it would be better if you left *Dinetah* now rather than later. I can lend you the money to get a fresh start somewhere else."

Stunned, Lexie blinked her eyes and took a moment, trying to decide what to say about his huge change in direction. Michael was studying her closely, probably waiting for her to break down again.

"I'm not evil and didn't do anything wrong," she finally managed. "We've been through this before and for the last time, I'm not leaving."

She'd said the words as calmly as possible and steeled herself to continue. "My son deserves to get to know his family and to learn about his heritage. I've decided Jack is staying. And I am certainly not going to walk away from my child."

Michael twisted back around to face the windshield

and cranked the ignition while he mumbled something under his breath. He no doubt must be thinking she was a stubborn and crazy white woman not to turn tail and run away.

But he didn't know about her mission. And he probably wouldn't believe her even if she told him.

Lexie had no place else to go. No place else calling her name where she was needed as much.

She and Jack were definitely staying. No matter what superstitious gossip was going around.

It seemed like only a few minutes later when Lexie felt the pickup straining to climb one of the mountain grades. The scenery out her window looked less and less like the desert she'd expected to see around Monument Valley and more and more like the pines and cedars near Michael's home.

"Where'd you say we were heading?"

"We're taking a small detour," he answered. "I've learned that the *hataalii* we seek for your Sing has gone on a pilgrimage to his birthplace in the mountains."

Lexie stared at him, feeling confused. "But I thought the more important part of our excursion today was trying to find those petroglyphs you've been talking about. The ones connected to the Skinwalkers."

"Both things are equally important. When the Sing is completed, the witch stigma will disappear and we can concentrate on finding the petroglyphs."

She raised her eyebrows, but didn't imagine he could see her while he watched the road. "You sure about the witch stuff going away after the Sing? I wonder if it will. And I can't help thinking your work finding the Skinwalker parchments has to be much more vital than any stupid gossip about an Anglo woman."

Michael forced himself to take a breath, waiting until the sudden and unusual burst of pride he'd just experienced faded away again. Lexie was beginning to care more about the Navajo and their war with the Skinwalkers than she did for herself. All his talking and lessons must be sinking in. She was coming around to the Navajo Way of harmony within self—and to the power of community.

Of course, he still couldn't stand the idea of her being ostracized or being in any physical danger due to the Skinwalkers. Intending to keep her safe, he vowed to continue searching for the old *hataalii* who could give her the blessing.

He glanced up at patches of blue sky peeking through the shelter of the pines above them. Here, high on the western slope of the mountains of his homeland, billowing clouds only hinted at the gloom he'd found in the valley below. True, a few thunderheads towered above lower cumulus clouds and were definitely fringed by rain shadows. But those distant harbingers of potential rainfall shouldn't cause them any trouble.

A break in the tension he'd been experiencing since early this morning finally allowed him to relax for a second. Normally optimistic, Michael was pleased to find himself once again believing everything would work out.

The Skinwalkers would be vanquished by the Brotherhood in the end. Lexie's unwanted visions of the ghosts would go away and leave her in peace. Jack would have the opportunity to learn the Way and grow closer to his clan. He and Lexie would somehow come to…

They would come to what? What did he want for their relationship? Where could they go together in the end?

Michael glanced up then and spotted the unmarked turnoff to Tocito Wash straight ahead. He guided his pickup onto the gravel road.

"How far do we have to go?" Lexie asked as they bounced along the washboard bumps.

"*Hastiin* Todacheene's maternal clan are *Tachiinii,* the Red-Running-into-the-Water Clan. Years ago, I spent time with them during a drought. My mother's clan helped them out by bringing hay in for the sheep during the emergency.

"I'm hoping I can remember where their hogan was located after all this time."

"Do you think it will take much longer to get there?"

He shot her a look. "Got someplace you have to be?"

Seeing a shiver tremble along the skin on her arms, Michael wished he could take back the smart remark. "What's up, Lexie? Aren't you feeling well?"

"I'm fine. But, well, I don't know. Something feels…off…all of a sudden."

As they rounded a sharp curve in the road, a family compound could be seen in the distance a quarter mile below them. It would take quite a while to reach the place due to the many switchbacks and the slow going on the gravel.

"We've got them in sight. See there?" As he pointed, it occurred to Michael he wasn't seeing any signs of life in the family's compound.

He had hoped Lexie would have a chance to get out of the truck to stretch, and he'd wanted the time himself to ask about the old *hataalii*. But no smoke coming from cookstove chimneys and no sign of animals in any of the pens told him those had been fruitless wishes.

Just then an ominous shadow came out of nowhere and threw darkness over the whole scene. Michael felt the evil like ants crawling across his spine.

But it was far too late to go back.

Chapter 10

Lexie turned her head when she heard his intake of breath and watched as Michael's whole body tensed. His hands gripped the steering wheel with white knuckles. His eyes narrowed on the road ahead.

"Is something the matter?"

He shook his head. "I'm not sure. Probably not."

Okay, now he was being just plain weird again.

"Well, I smell something…funny." Lexie wrinkled her nose as she sniffed the air.

Michael slowed the truck. "Funny, how?"

"Um. Like barbecue."

Michael rolled down his window and sniffed. "I don't smell anything. You can't be hungry again. It hasn't been two hours since you had breakfast."

"Which *you* didn't let me finish," Lexie said with a

scowl. "For your information, I'm not hungry. But it does smell like something's cooking."

The damn man was doing it again. He was being insufferable.

Lexie turned to stare out her window, folded her arms over her chest and decided to sulk until they reached the house they'd seen from back up the mountain. Wasn't it bad enough that she'd had to face a Skinwalker Bear and then had someone threaten her with words drawn in paint on the side of Michael's truck? Apparently not. She also had to suffer through an interminable ride down the mountainside with an arrogant jerk who claimed to be alert to everything but her.

They ought not be here at all. If it had been up to her, they'd be in the desert trying to find the cave with the petroglyphs. Not on some wild-goose chase, looking for an elusive medicine man who might or might not exist.

In fifteen minutes Michael pulled up in the yard of the house they'd seen, but it didn't look like anyone was home.

"Is it possible they've gone shopping and will be back today?" she asked as they both sat quietly in their seats.

"Maybe. But highly unlikely. The weeds have grown up in the paths and the windows are clogged with sand and pine needles. There aren't any sheep in the pens. It might be they've taken the sheep to winter pasture, but it's awfully early in the season."

They sat in the truck another five minutes in absolute silence with Michael sitting stiff and alert.

Finally she couldn't stand it anymore. "Why don't you knock on the door? Do you think they'd mind if we climbed down from the truck for a moment to kick out the kinks?" She reached for the door handle.

"Navajos don't knock at a hogan. They wait to be invited in."

Opening her door and leaving it ajar, she turned back for a second. "I'm going to walk around the pickup for a while. I won't go near the house until I'm invited."

She jumped down and closed the door. But when she came around the pickup, Michael was standing right before her.

"Okay," he said. "You stay here by the truck then. I want to check on something around the other side of the hogan." He took off at a good clip through the tall weeds.

Heck no, she wasn't going to stay here all by herself. Lexie raced to catch up. "What are you going to check?"

He frowned as she kept pace beside him. "The front of the house faces east. I need to see the north side."

"Why?" she asked breathlessly. He really needed to slow down.

"It's possible someone died here and the family abandoned the place."

"Abandoned?"

"In the old traditions, if someone dies inside a hogan their *chindi* will be stuck in that place. The rest of the clan will prepare and bury the body close by, then knock a hole in the north facing wall hoping the evil spirit will leave. After that the family will go away for good."

"But what if the *chindi* does leave? Can the family come back?"

He shook his head. "They won't. No matter what."

Just then, the two of them turned the corner of the house and found a completely intact north wall. "Looks like no one's died here," Lexie said with an out of breath huff.

Michael ran his hands through his hair and looked frustrated. "I don't understand it. I was so sure…"

As his words dropped off, Lexie began hearing a strange noise coming from somewhere higher up the mountainside behind them. It sounded like crackling cellophane, punctuated occasionally by another noise sounding more like someone popping those little air pillows that make up clear plastic packing material used to wrap breakables. She'd done that kind of popping herself. It was kind of addictive.

"Michael…"

He turned a frustrated gaze in her direction. "What? I don't know what we should do next. Or where to look—"

"But Michael," she interrupted, growing alarmed. "Don't you hear that noise?"

"What noise?" He swung around, standing still to listen.

At that moment, his whole demeanor changed. She watched him straighten, while his body snapped to attention.

"Move!" he shouted as he suddenly grabbed her arm and began to run.

"What is it?" she screamed back as they dashed together toward the pickup.

"Fire. Coming right at us. Get in the truck now!"

Rounding the corner of the house, she looked up the road past the pickup. To her horror, the whole side of the mountain appeared to be ablaze. Everything, all the pines and cedars they'd driven through, every bit of it was burning while the flames licked and jumped from tree to tree. It seemed as if the fire was headed right for them, just like he'd said. A wall of fire raced down along the edge of the gravel road they'd traveled.

They made it to the pickup, jumped in and turned the engine over in ten seconds flat.

"Where are we going?" she asked as they buckled up in record time. "We can't go back."

"We have to outrun it. But the road peters out another half mile down the valley."

"Then what?"

"Then we hope this pickup can make it through the rocks and sand to the wash a mile or so beyond. There should be water running in the wash after those rains we had."

As they drove past the hogan, outbuildings and pens, Lexie heard Michael begin chanting under his breath. She hoped whatever he was singing could stop a fire, because if not they were in a whole world of trouble.

And she was most definitely *not* ready to die today.

Michael clung to the steering wheel as they bumped and bounced off the gravel and down the rocky slope. He hoped he'd guessed right about the direction of the wash. The last time he'd been there was at least fifteen years ago.

Swinging the wheel to the left around a patch of tamarisk trees and buffalo berry sheep food, he noticed the sky above them was growing dark again. The wind had changed and was blowing the black smoke in their direction.

He didn't dare push the truck any more than he already had. One wrong move and they'd either head off the edge of a twenty-foot drop or become stuck in shifting sand.

"Can you reach my phone?"

Lexie spun to look at him. Her eyes were wild and her whole body was tense.

"Where is it?" she said through chattering teeth.

"In my jacket pocket. We need to report the fire. Maybe the firefighters can bring a helicopter out here to rescue us."

She leaned to look up at the thick smoke above the truck and shook her head. "Do you think they could land through all that?"

"Try calling."

Ducking under her own seat belt and reaching all the way around him, she managed to get the phone out of his pocket. But not before bumping her chin on the wheel a few times.

She sat back in her seat, while he gave instructions on which phone buttons to push. She did it, listened for a second then turned to look at him with alarm in her eyes.

"There's no signal. Nothing's happening."

Michael said a few cusswords in Navajo. What good was having brand-new Brotherhood satellite phones if the signal couldn't get out from under thick layers of smoke?

"Never mind," he spat out as he battled to keep the truck from spinning in the sand. "Sit tight. We'll get ourselves out of this."

Managing to keep them from disaster, he began spotting drainages as they careened down the mountainside. Which meant the wash could not be far ahead. The thick clouds of smoke had broken up somewhat, too, leaving patchy skies above them. Maybe they were going to make it after all.

Finally, with the pickup barely edging over the last rough patch, he found himself heading down into the steepest canyon yet. There right below them, streaming swiftly over the gravel bottom, was a few feet of real running water. He couldn't remember a nicer sight.

"I see the water," Lexie exclaimed. "But how is it going to save us?"

"We'll see," he said, trying to maintain his calm. "But first we're going in. The truck needs cooling off. I've been smelling the tires burning for quite a while."

He'd known metal, rubber and the engine had been overheating from the intense fire. But for the last few minutes, he'd become more concerned about spontaneous combustion.

Driving right into the twelve-foot-wide stretch of water, Michael imagined he could hear the actual sizzle of metal cooling. But then, because he'd turned the pickup broadside in the stream, the fast-running current began buffeting them.

"Oh," Lexie gulped. She reached out to steady herself with both hands on the dashboard.

He stepped on the gas and fought the wheel again, this time swinging the pickup downstream. Not liking the idea of being stuck in this narrow canyon when the fire arrived and raged over their heads, Michael wasn't sure what his next move should be. The water's current was flowing too hard at the moment for him drive across to the far side. His only choice for now seemed to be continuing downstream. But he didn't like staying in this narrow canyon.

The sky turned dark again and he heard the roar of wildfire over the sounds of engine and rushing water.

They weren't making fast enough headway to outrun the flames.

Stopping, he threw the truck into park and turned to Lexie. "I think our best bet is to get out and run for it."

"Run? Where to?"

"Downstream. Until we find a cleft in the canyon where we can climb the far rim."

"But the truck. Our stuff?"

"We'll carry what we can." He shut off the engine and unbuckled. "But we have to go *now*."

Lexie turned to look behind them. Then turned back to him with barely concealed panic written across her face.

"If you say so." She unbuckled and inched open her door. "Damn. I can't believe I'm in the middle of a flood again and in a vehicle with the water rising. Didn't I just go through this same thing?"

"Come my way," he told her as he pushed open his own door. "I'll help you."

The water was barely lapping at the running boards, but he figured she deserved a break. He lifted her out of the driver's side and carried her to the far bank before returning for their things in the truck's bed. After making two trips for as much as he thought they could carry, it was time to go.

Each of them began loading up. As fast as he could, he tied a duffel onto Lexie's back with a braided rope so she could use her hands for other things. Then he did the same for himself before they set off walking along the bank, heading downstream.

It was slow going with heavy packs, scrambling over gravel and the occasional boulder. After a few hundred yards, the canyon walls seemed to be widening out, becoming less steep. Good for climbing out, terrible if the fire reached them first.

He urged her to go faster. In about another mile they rounded an abrupt bend in the canyon and he spotted a stone hogan on their side of the wash. The place had been built high enough up the slope to be safe from potential flash floods. And he could see a natural path that would make an easy climb up from the canyon floor.

"That's our way out," he told Lexie.

They staggered up the path to the rim and found the second abandoned hogan they'd visited today. This one wasn't as neat as the other. The roof was made of tar paper with a rusty chimney pipe sticking out of the center. There was also a lopsided shed, a tiny animal pen and an old outhouse on the property.

Not much to look at. But it would shelter them from the sun while they rested and decided what to do next.

"No one's here," Lexie said as they came close. "Do you think someone died?"

He shook his head. "There's no hole in the north side. I would imagine these people have taken their sheep down to flatter ground for the coming winter. This is rough territory and it may take weeks to get the animals moved from here."

"Is there a chance the fire could reach us up here on this side of the water?"

"It's wide enough here, I doubt the fire would be able to jump the canyon in this spot."

"Then do you think they'd mind if we stayed for a little while?"

She really did look beat. Her nose had turned pink from the sun and she was bent under the strain of her pack.

"I think they would invite us in to rest. That's the Navajo Way. I'll bet they don't even lock their doors."

He tried the door, calling out as it opened with a creak. "See there. Let's get out of the sun."

Inside, the place was not much to look at, either. With an old cookstove in the middle of the room, blankets and sheepskins lining one wall and shelves with foodstuffs lining the other, it was minimalism at its finest. But the place had an actual plank board floor instead of dirt, and it was spotless. He helped Lexie unload what she'd been carrying, handed her the canteen and then spread a sheepskin out for her to sit down.

She took a drink, eased down on the sheepskin and looked up at him. "Thanks. Do you think your phone will work from here? Maybe we can call for help now."

Reaching into his pocket and finding nothing, Michael shook his head with chagrin. "Maybe we *could've* called if I had my phone. I'm not sure where I lost it. But we're safe here while we figure out our next move. Don't worry."

Telling her not to worry had been easier to say than it would be for him to do. They were safe, he would make sure of it. But he didn't want Lexie to know there might be plenty left to worry about. So he plastered on a smile and tried to think of ways for them to get out of here while he searched through the cans for something to eat.

Lexie awoke, sat up and looked around, trying to gain her bearings. It took a second to remember that she'd been taking a nap after they'd finished their meal. Michael had mixed up canned tomatoes and beans, threw in some dried peppers and cooked it all in a frying pan along with a little canned meat. Then he'd encouraged her to rest during the hottest part of the day.

But where was he now?

She got up and opened the hogan's door, not sure of what she would find. Thrilled to discover the sky was clear and without a trace of smoke, she took a deep breath. There was a slight lingering smell of burning brush in the air, but she didn't feel the same threat of fire as before.

Concerned about Michael, Lexie found him outside saying a chant just as the sky was beginning to show early signs of a robust sunset. Crimson and plum streaks shot out around the edges of the western mountains, making for a spectacular display against an indigo sky.

Waiting until he'd stopped singing and looked up at her, Lexie asked, "What's the chant for?"

"I'm protecting the hogan and surroundings against Skinwalkers." He looked away a split second, then met her gaze straight on. "I haven't found a way to get you out of here just yet. We'll have to spend the night. If something doesn't change by tomorrow morning, though, I'll walk out to the nearest neighbor with a phone."

"How far will you have to go?"

He shrugged. "I'm not positive. Maybe as much as twenty miles since I have no idea exactly which direction."

Twenty miles? Lexie didn't know what to say. All of sudden their situation looked desperate.

Michael grinned at her. "Don't look so grim. It's me that'll be walking. I'll leave you with plenty of food and water. You'll be fine."

When Lexie still couldn't get her mouth open wide

enough to speak, he suddenly changed the subject. "Since you're awake now, I've rigged up a sun shower if you'd like to clean up a bit. But you'll have to use it soon before the sun drops behind the mountaintops."

"A shower? For real?"

"Close enough. I brought soap along in my backpack and there's water and a hose arrangement from the well."

"You're on," she told him. "Can I wash my shirt and underwear while I'm at it?"

The expression on his face was a riot. She could've sworn the great professor-slash-medicine man was embarrassed. Then after a second, she watched as electricity took over and heat sprung up in his eyes. Heat and hunger. It made her burn with a sudden flash of desire, just by looking at him.

He cleared his throat—twice. "Do you have something to change into while it dries? I could lend you the extra T-shirt I brought along. But I don't have any...any underwear that you..."

She waved away his concern and his embarrassed stuttering. "The T-shirt will be great. Thanks."

The luxury of feeling clean put Lexie in a much better mood. By the time the sun disappeared and dusk was nearly finished creeping along the cliffs, she was drying off and ready for almost anything.

She went looking for Michael and found him in front of the hogan airing out a couple of sheepskins. "Can I help?"

Swinging around in her direction, he opened his mouth, took one sharp look at her and turned away again. "What the devil happened to your jeans?"

"They smelled like smoke. I rinsed them out and hung them up with my other stuff."

With his back still turned to her, he nodded. "I see."

"But I'm perfectly decent. This T-shirt you gave me comes all the way down to my knees."

"Right," he said as he brushed past her holding the sheepskins between them like a shield.

Lexie followed him into the hogan. "My clothes should air-dry fairly quickly in this low humidity even without the sun. I'll be able to put them back on in the morning."

"That isn't the point."

Without so much as a glance in her direction, he spread the sheepskins out on the hogan floor. One set of skins he placed in the southernmost corner and the other set in the northernmost corner.

He pointed to the north corner of the hogan. "That side's yours. Males sit and sleep on the southern side."

When he seemed satisfied the nests he'd made would be as comfortable as possible, he stirred the fire in the cookstove and finally turned. "And the real *point* is that I have to stay near you tonight for your protection. But I can't even look at you without imagining what you're like with nothing on under that T-shirt."

Well, what do you know? He was finally—finally—admitting out loud the sensual draw so evident between them. Lexie immediately felt the draw herself as her nipples peaked against his T-shirt and a wet heat sprung up between her legs. She took a step in his direction.

"Don't," he told her. "It isn't going to happen."

He brushed past her again and headed out into the twilight. She followed him, trying to keep her anger and desire from getting the better of her. She would not beg the man to make love to her.

When she came up behind him, he was leaning against a low fence staring up at the many red dots of light on the mountainside. "Is that the fire?" she asked to his back.

"Yes, but it appears to be receding. I suspect the Navajo Nation's firefighters got a handle on it this afternoon. Maybe by tomorrow the worst of the fire will be contained. That should make things easier for us."

She thought not being threatened by the fire might make things simpler for them to get out of here, but leaving would do nothing to make things easier between the two of them. They needed to talk about their desires and hungers.

"Michael…" she began, not knowing how to approach the subject but desperate to find a way.

"Go back inside and go to bed. There's nothing to do without electricity after dark except for sleeping. Morning comes early here on the eastern slope of the mountains. By then we can decide how best to get out of this place."

The damned man wouldn't even talk to her about how best to deal with their desires. Furious with him for cutting off any discussion—and furious with herself for wanting him anyway—she spun around and stormed into the hogan, slamming the door behind her.

She lay down on the sheepskins and closed her eyes, positive she was way too angry and wide-awake to ever fall asleep. The next thing she knew, her eyes blinked open and she realized the fire in the cookstove had gone out. How long had she been asleep and what time was it?

Sitting up, she listened carefully and heard soft snoring coming from the southern corner. It was too dark to see much but she imagined Michael must've come in after she'd gone to sleep and settled into his own spot.

Wide-awake now, Lexie needed a breath of air. She also needed to back away from the growing temptation to crawl right beside him and let the heat take them where it would.

She forced herself toward the door, which they'd left standing ajar for the moonlight, and silently closed it behind her. If he didn't want her, she would find the strength not to want him.

Once outside, she was struck by the spectacular isolation and the beauty of the stars without any electric lights to obscure their brilliance. Walking to the same fence Michael had leaned against earlier, she marveled at the sheer vastness of the earth and the enormity of the universe above their heads.

The night sky made her feel a part of humanity. Yet in another way, it also made her feel isolated and alone.

Just then, she heard the creak of the door and knew Michael must've awoken and come outside to find her. But she refused to turn around and acknowledge the damned man.

Minutes of silence went by and she wondered where he'd gone. Before she could surrender and call out to him, she heard—no, maybe she only *sensed* his presence behind her. He made no sounds at all, yet his warmth and scent were close enough to send sensual chills up her spine.

Okay, then. This time she vowed he would *not* back away until she'd had her chance to talk.

Chapter 11

She turned, ready to make him listen for once. But when she found him standing over her in the bright moonlight, the expression on his face said more than any words could. She could see desperation painted in those eyes. Desperation that had changed him from an arrogant professor into a man with enormous needs and wants. Both her words and muscles failed as she froze and stared up at him.

Only able to focus on his eyes, she imagined they were speaking to her—mesmerizing her.

The desert night air encased them in a private cocoon. For long minutes, no sounds disturbed their world. No wind, no night noises. Then from a distance a bird screeched and a coyote called. Still, Michael never flinched nor made any move to back away. His gaze held her in a tight prison of the senses.

As the wind began picking up, a dark cloud swirled

above their heads. Like him, Lexie never moved a muscle as she stared up through the moonlight into his eyes. Then something flickered between them and anticipation flipped a switch of heat inside her body. There was a wildness in the air, as a static charge lifted and frizzed her hair, leaving her dangling on the teetering edge of danger.

The two of them remained where they were—caught in some warp of a magic night. She'd thought at first he might kiss her. Now she silently begged him to. Begged him with a gaze to stop her tension and growing need.

Instead of bending to kiss her, though, he lifted his hand and used a thumb to rub across her lips. Steady and slow. Achingly slow. The friction was glorious. And then it was hell as the charge ran along her skin and torched her nerve endings.

Wanting him to touch her and needing him to put an end to this standoff, her frustration grew to monumental proportions. Tremendous heat rolled through every body part, and the tiny hairs on her arms and the back of her neck prickled until she at last retreated from the extreme tension. She dropped her gaze down his body only to find him bare-chested. Why hadn't she noticed?

The sight of those broad, bare shoulders, the ones she'd only been able to guess at before, threw her even further into an erotic recklessness. Those rippling chest muscles devoid of hair. The toned, bronze-colored biceps. The sexy picture he made half-naked went far beyond her imagination. Her throat went dry and a drop of perspiration rolled down her temple.

She couldn't breathe, couldn't move and finally she couldn't take any more.

Turning her back to him, she tried to steady herself enough to find her voice. What was he doing out here without saying a word? Why hadn't he made a move? Stay or go. Something had to give soon.

With a whisper of rustling air, she felt him close the small gap between them. Just as she was going to turn around and meet his silence with questions, Lexie felt his palms settle on her hips. Those hot, large hands that held her pinned in place, caused what was left of her mind to spin in wild imaginings.

Still without saying anything, she picked up on his erratic breathing, felt the heat of it steaming through her hair. Fisting her hands, she bit her tongue to keep from saying anything until he did. Her heart rate increased as he pulled her back against the hard pressure of his erection.

Starting to feel light-headed from the combination of erotic silence and breathtaking frustration, she wondered if he was trying to torture her. Would she pass out from the intensity of it?

Then he made his move. She jumped as his mouth came down on her damp neck and his hands shifted upward to her ultrasensitive breasts. Hearing him growl, she went nuts as the sound came out low and urgent, from somewhere deep within his chest. Feral, she thought. Raw and primitive.

It was all so suddenly savage and thrilling her head started to spin. She worried about reaching a peak too soon. No one had ever taken her this high this fast. Tilting her head slightly to give him better access, she fought to hold back the billowing internal explosion threatening to end it all.

Heat from his palms seared right through the T-shirt she wore. Massaging her breasts until each peak was wound painfully tight, he pulled and pinched each nipple in turn until she thought she would go crazy.

Then she noticed he'd only been using one hand. That thought hit her just as his other hand glided upward under the T-shirt and palmed her bottom. The sensation of hot skin against hot skin shimmered through her, becoming velvet fire.

Lexie's eyelids grew heavy. But she could swear she saw shooting stars as they strobed across a silken sky.

Then Michael's other hand spread out wide, encompassing the material covering her belly. He inched that hand lower, until it, too, found its way under the T-shirt. With her naked lower torso caught tightly between his two palms, the skin there heated as if it had been scorched by flames. In moments, her very womb began to boil and her knees turned to melted butter.

She managed to brace herself against the wooden fence railing and stayed upright, but she was waging a full-out internal war. Battling the intense desire to turn around and reach for him. Fighting the insistent urge to scream out his name. Most of all, she desperately tried to hold the coming pinnacle and make this heaven and hell last.

When his fingers slid between her thighs, Lexie feared the jolt might just blow the top of her head off. She opened her eyes wide but stopped breathing, waiting for his next move.

She didn't have long to wait. Holding her steady by biting down on her neck, he began stroking and kneading the flesh on both her buttocks and the inside of her thighs. His sensual movements were sending her off to some kind of higher plane. A place where pain and pleasure mixed and became fantasy.

When she felt a sudden rush of warm wetness between her legs, his calloused thumbs touched the opening to her most sensitive spot. She moaned, squirmed involuntarily. She heard him groan, too, then before she knew what he'd intended, he'd lifted the T-shirt up and over her head.

Feeling him kneel behind her, she quieted, stunned at what he was doing. His warm breath began reheating the already sensitive skin of her buttocks. Dazed and confused, and so crazed with desire she could barely breathe, she had no choice but to give herself over to him.

Gently, almost tenderly, he used his thumbs to spread her legs. In a trance, she accommodated him by adjusting her stance. Lexie couldn't quite understand what he wanted and felt a flush of embarrassment, knowing he was staring at her normally hidden places up close. Then, she felt him touch the tip of his finger to the pulsating spot that ached the most for attention. Moments later, his finger moved inside her and set off the explosion she had tried so hard to hold back.

Everything felt so foreign and yet so erotic and satisfying that it had pushed her right over the cliff. She hadn't wanted to go alone, but found it impossible to hold in the scream of pleasure, let alone hold back the rising tides of her release.

She felt sultry and lethargic now but Michael apparently was moving fast behind her. Through her smoky, lusty haze, she heard a zipper lower. Next she was bent forward in the middle as he pushed at her back.

Gripping her tightly around the waist, he plunged inside her with one swift movement. The sensation of being pervaded by him drew her up again, drove sparks along all her nerve endings and awakened all her senses.

He stilled, waiting as her body stretched and allowed him greater access. After only a moment, he began a slow stroke, filling her and sending her senses soaring. How could she so soon be back on that tight edge again? Never before had anyone…

Gulping for air, she heard him doing the same. But his rhythm remained steady, until tension curled so tightly in her gut she thought she might physically come apart and implode this time.

His thrusts increased then, growing to a frantic and furious pace. She stayed with him all the way, reveling in the way his muscles hardened to steel. In an amazing feat, he brought them both to the boundary of their erotic universe as one.

Strobe lights started up behind her closed eyelids, as her entire body shattered into a trillion pieces. Lost in a personal shower of electricity and shooting stars, this time she let currents take her wherever they would.

Michael regulated his breathing and waited to hear Lexie do the same. He was determined not to move a muscle, to keep her tightly within his arms until he was sure she was okay. But his knees were shaky. His body still vibrated from the savage pleasure he'd taken from her.

What had he done? Had the primitive animal, who'd taken her out in the open without so much as one kiss, really been him? He'd never done anything so intensely crazy in his entire life.

He didn't regret one instant. But how would he explain his insanity to her? He couldn't say, "Sorry, but the mere sight of you standing under the stars in nothing but my T-shirt drove me crazy." And he wouldn't tell her that the bone-deep pleasure of dipping his fingers into her heat and wetness had been enough to make a grown man cry. Nor could he gather enough courage to say he never would've been able to go through with it at all if he'd had to face her.

Just seeing her looking up at him as he took her, knowing she would think him a traitor to her husband's memory, would have stopped him cold.

It wasn't something he could ever explain. To her, or to himself. But he would never forget it.

Where did that leave them now, though? His harsh and inconsiderate moves may even have cost them a friendship. What's more, without the first thought toward protection, his errors may well end up bringing her more trouble than she could handle. Lexie was adept at being a single mother to *one* half-Navajo child. But two?

Michael felt her stirring beneath him. Her jerky movements began to revive passion in a man who thought he must surely be too exhausted for anything more tonight.

He tried to ignore the returning heat in his body, and swore there would be no more accidents or savagery on his account. Especially not out here under the open canopy of the cosmos where anyone could spot them.

Finding a steadier footing, he straightened up, taking her with him. She nearly collapsed as her knees gave out, so he swung her up in his arms and headed for the hogan, determined once again to protect her—even if it had to be from himself.

Kicking open the hogan door, Michael gently lowered her naked body down on top of the nest of sheepskins he'd made for her earlier. He quickly moved away from temptation and toward his own corner, all the while wondering how they could ever go back to working together tomorrow.

But then, in the low glow of moonlight, he saw Lexie open her eyes and reach out to him. "Stay. Don't walk away. Just please hold me."

How could he say no to anything she asked of him? Even knowing touching her right now would not be a good idea, he nevertheless went back and lay down beside her, gathering her close. Because she'd asked him to.

She rolled tightly against his body and buried her face in his neck with a moan. His insides twisted and hardened again. His whole body flashed back to attention.

An impossible situation was about to get a whole lot worse.

Throughout the rise and fall of the night's full moon, they reached for each other again and again. All his vows of protection and all his swearing to be more careful simply disappeared whenever she whispered his name.

He was bound to pay a dear price for all this pleasure. His harmony and balance would definitely be affected badly by such unbridled passion with a woman who didn't belong to him. But he'd be damned if he could worry about that in the face of her desire.

Swimming up from some weird dreamless sleep, Michael cracked open his eyes and found dawn already streaming through the windows and the open door. He turned his head to look for Lexie and spotted her standing over the cookstove in the middle of the one big room.

She had on his T-shirt again and appeared to be readying something to cook. He held his breath for the moment and took in the gorgeous, sleep-tossed sight of her.

"What're you doing?" he asked as he sat up and reached for the jeans he'd thrown aside in the middle of the night.

"Fixing mush…or I will be as soon as the water boils. I watched your mother preparing mush the other day. And when I found an old mayonnaise jar filled with ground blue cornmeal, I thought I'd give it a try."

Michael felt his heart skip a beat. "You know how to use a wood-fired cookstove?" This was a very special woman and he was absolutely crazy about her.

She smiled. "Sure. Dan and I lived in Alaska for few months one winter. Everyone there learns or freezes."

Those words stopped him, reminding him of the many mistakes he'd already made with her. With his brother's widow, dammit. What a complete imbecile he was.

However, Lexie didn't look as if she was the least bit miserable or feeling ashamed the way he was. Instead, she most resembled a woman who had happily made love throughout the night, and who now was fixing breakfast for the very man who had made her so happy.

That thought made him completely lose his appetite. What in hell was he going to do with all these unchecked emotions? All the guilt. The lust. The love. The love?

His stomach rolled. When had the practical, intelligent man he'd always thought himself to be disappeared? Well whenever it was, he desperately needed to find his old familiar self, the man who didn't love or lust uncontrollably, once again.

"I'm sure whatever you fix will be terrific," he told her as he shoved his arms into his flannel long-sleeved shirt. "But I think I'd better make plans to get away from here before the sun gets too high. I also want to check on the wildfire. See if it's still smoldering."

"You're not thinking of starting the twenty-mile walk without even eating, are you?"

Shaking his head and turning his back, he was not able to look at her without taking her in his arms. He needed time. He needed space. He needed a brain transplant.

"I thought first I'd go back and check on the pickup," he muttered over his shoulder. "See how much damage the fire caused. Maybe some miracle saved my phone.

"But you go ahead and eat something," he added as he pulled on his boots. "Then change clothes and start packing up. I've decided, whatever way we choose to get out of here, we're going to go together."

More than an hour later, Lexie was beginning to worry. What was taking Michael so long? She tried to kept the tiny frisson of panic she'd been battling out of her mind. But what would she do if something happened to him?

She finished tying her boots and decided to walk down the steep slope to see if she could find him. After a few trying yards of slipping on the gravel rocks, Lexie came to a stop and leaned over, peering downward into the wash.

But Michael wasn't anywhere in sight. She'd almost turned back when she spotted something that nearly floored her. The rushing water in the bottom of the wash had become a mere trickle.

That was good, wasn't it? Maybe now they could follow the wash downstream instead of either trying to strike out across the arid mesa to a neighbor's or fighting backward the way they'd come through still smoldering forests. She wondered how far this wash actually went before it ran into other homes or a town. Such a good source of water *must* hit civilization eventually.

She would just have to wait and ask Michael to be sure. There was no sense letting her nerves push her into doing something rash like leaving without him just because he was late. He'd be back in a while. Nothing could possibly happen to him. Not when he was so strong, so intelligent, so—sexy.

Oh boy, what a damned, dumb woman she was, Lexie chided herself. She'd been doing her level best not to think about the terrific sex they'd shared last night. Michael apparently hadn't even wanted to bring it up this morning. She'd never seen anyone so anxious to get away from her after he'd awoken. He'd practically run out the door the minute he opened his eyes.

But he certainly was in *her* thoughts, and had been for every single minute since she'd awoken this morning. What they'd done together came back to her in erotic flashes when she least expected them. The two of them had shared something more than just sensual— more even than simply beautiful and intense. It had been way beyond her experience.

And it wasn't going to ever happen again. At least it had better not. She couldn't seem to shake the aftereffects. Even now, hours later, her body still burned and she still felt needy and desperate for his touch.

He obviously didn't feel the same. So that was that.

Still, last night he'd seemed so solicitous. Her mind went right back to dwelling on him, despite her best intentions. He'd been gentle and loving. Well, all right, so he'd also been savage and a little rough. But that was only what she'd wanted him to be. He'd done everything in the way she'd imagined a dream lover would. That had been why she'd been so sure he must really care for her. Then.

This morning everything had changed. The arrogant professor who apparently wanted the crazy psychic to be cured just so she could leave his territory had been back in his eyes. Her sexy warrior lover had disappeared along with the night.

She'd learned a lesson. A hard lesson. Never let yourself go with a man who refuses to talk. This morning she felt lonely and sort of guilty—and she wasn't about to let that happen again.

Silently berating herself, she turned away from the wash and headed back up the slope to wait for him. He'd get here whenever he got here. As he'd told her once, she needed more patience.

When Lexie reached the level ground, she halted in place at an odd and slightly scary sight. A middle-aged Navajo woman dressed in modern clothes seemed to be quietly waiting for her near the hogan.

Startled but not afraid, because Michael had promised the place was protected from Skinwalkers and evil, Lexie walked closer to the woman. She sure hoped this lady knew a little English.

"Ya'at'eeh," the Navajo woman said.

"Hi. Do you live around here?"

"No, daughter-in-law of the Big Medicine Clan. I have come only to offer advice. To give directions and messages to the new Message Bearer."

Lexie couldn't help the shudder that ran along her backbone. Heavens. This wasn't a neighbor coming to their aid, it was another ghostly spirit. Very probably another of Michael and Dan's relatives.

She tried to give the ghost a half smile. Maybe her advice and message would be about how to find their way out of this place.

"Can I get you anything?" she asked for lack of knowing what was proper. "A cup of water?"

The woman shook her head and smiled.

Lexie wondered at how stupid she could possibly be to offer water to a ghost But, she sure wished she had something to drink herself. Her throat had gone dry and raspy at the very idea of hearing from one more ghost.

"You know who I was in life," the ghost told her. "I was known as the Plant Tender during my time in this world."

"Oh?" *Ooohhh.* Michael had said his aunt, Shirley Nez, the Old Plant Tender, had been killed by Skinwalkers. This must be her. Another chill skipped through Lexie's veins.

"My nephew has strayed from the correct path. He lets his heart rule his head. I have come asking for your help to set him straight again."

Michael letting his heart rule his head? That sure didn't sound like the arrogant professor Lexie knew.

"The man you love has the power to find the answers," the ghost began again.

The man she *what?* No way. She did not love Michael Ayze. Not even a little bit. No doubt that he'd been a terrific and sensitive lover. But he was a hell of a long way from being a man she could really *love*. When and if she ever loved a man again, that man would be able to talk to her openly and easily.

"Look, I don't—" she began.

The ghost broke through her denial with a slight shake of her head. "Lead him to the desert. To the place he'd meant to search. Today. I will give you directions to make it easier to find the way."

"Today?" If they actually got the heck out of this remote wilderness today, all Lexie wanted was to find Jack and hold him in her arms. And then she wanted to take a nice long nap.

"Wasted moments bring a bigger potential for disaster."

Okay, Lexie understood they were in a war and war required sacrifices, but there might be yet another problem. "What if he won't listen to me? I tried to tell him before not to go nuts looking for some old medicine man guy that might not still be alive."

"He will listen now."

If so, it would be the first miracle Lexie would ever witness. "I'll try."

The ghost told her the directions then, and Lexie made herself memorize every word. She refused to do a bad job in her first real assignment as the Message Bearer.

When the ghost finished talking, Lexie thought of something else. "What if we get chased again? Or what if someone tries to hurt us because they think I'm a witch?"

"By the time the sun sets tomorrow you will find the answer," the ghost said with another smile. "Listen to your lover. Then listen to your own heart."

Lexie opened her mouth to ask more questions about how to get out of the witchcraft business and about how to make Michael pay attention, but right then she heard an odd noise coming from down in the wash and turned to listen. It sounded like...

An engine? Could that be?

She spun back, but the ghost was gone. Inching her way down the slope again, Lexie got to where she could see into the wash below. After a moment of standing there staring toward the noise that seemed to be coming from upstream, she saw something big as it appeared at the sharp bend in the wash.

Her heart began beating so hard she thought she might faint, until she realized it was Michael's red pickup, making its way along the rutted and almost dry wash bottom. The truck was still running. They were saved.

Chapter 12

"You'd rather go straight to the desert and *not* stop to see Jack first? But you haven't seen him in over twenty-four hours." Michael eased down on the gas, tensed as he felt the tires slipping against the rocks on the wash bottom, then relaxed again as they caught traction and moved the pickup forward.

He was worried about Lexie. After he'd found the pickup in good shape and his phone high and dry, he'd thought she would jump at the chance to go back to civilization. Instead, the minute the pickup had been loaded with their stuff and the hogan cleaned and closed, she'd begun begging him to travel in the opposite direction, off to Monument Valley to look for petroglyphs.

"We could use your phone to call Jack at your sister's, couldn't we?" she hedged, and he noticed her plea for understanding. "As long as I can hear my boy's voice and know he's okay, I think I can wait a little longer to see him in person."

Michael shook his head. "What's gotten into you?"

Shooting her a quick glance, he saw a mixture of frustration and guilt in her eyes. And he wondered why.

"I have something to tell you," she said quietly.

A flash of his own guilt jolted him, set his nerves on edge. He gathered his wits and reminded himself it was too early for her to know if she was pregnant or not. The next second he also found himself swallowing a little disappointment. Wouldn't it be to his advantage if she were expecting a child?

Yeah, the idea of becoming a father and marrying Lexie suddenly sounded very appealing.

Clamping his mouth shut, he gave her a sharp go-ahead nod and waited for whatever she had to say.

"More ghosts have come to see me."

"What?" That was the last thing he'd thought she would say. It was the last thing he'd wanted to hear.

"Now don't get all huffy and don't raise your voice. These ghosts were *your* relatives."

"Mine? What the hell?" He put his foot on the brake and brought the truck to a stop. Turning, he faced her and waited for an explanation he didn't really want to hear.

She met his glare with one of her own and folded her arms over her chest. "This morning a Navajo woman's ghost came to see me. She told me she'd been known as the Plant Tender during her lifetime."

"My aunt, Shirley Nez?" Then Michael remembered Shirley's ghost had come to speak to his cousin Ben during a sweat bath vision quest a couple of years ago. He guessed there was a possibility her spirit might still be around to talk to Lexie. But it wasn't something he liked thinking about for very long.

"Yes," Lexie answered. "Apparently I'm going to be useful to the Brotherhood in the Skinwalker war. I'm supposed to act as the *Message Bearer.*"

"I've never even heard of such a person," he said without thinking. "And, believe me, I've learned every legend and story in the Navajo history. Exactly what kind of messages would you bring? And who are you supposed to tell?"

For the first time since they'd been stuck out here after the fire, Lexie set her jaw and seemed in total control. He wanted to reach out to her. To soothe and protect. But he didn't think his attentions would be wanted. Perhaps because of what he'd done last night.

"I'm supposed to tell *you,*" she told him. "Your aunt said you have the power to find the answers."

Oh, man. Michael felt the interior of the truck's cab closing in on him. He didn't want Lexie talking to ghosts. Such things were outside the Navajo Way and would only bring her trouble. But if Shirley Nez was really trying to communicate with the Brotherhood through Lexie, he couldn't afford to stop her. They needed all the help they could get to conquer the Skinwalkers.

He drew a breath, tried to settle his mind around having the woman he might love bringing messages from the ghost world. And maybe talking to Skinwalker *chindi.* The idea kept throwing his mind out of harmony.

Leaning his forehead against the steering wheel for just a moment's reflection, he cleared his thoughts. He knew the Old Plant Tender, his aunt, could not have left any bad spirits when she'd died. Shirley was the best person he'd ever known.

So perhaps if Lexie was to talk only to the spirit of Shirley Nez, she wouldn't come in contact with bad *chindi*. Could that be the answer? He needed more time to reason out the concepts.

"Are you feeling all right?" Lexie asked, bringing him around to the present.

He lifted his head and tried a smile. "Do you have a message to give me?"

Lexie nodded. "We're supposed to go to the desert today. Near the place you'd wanted to search for the petroglyphs."

"There are dozens of possibilities around that area we'll need to check," he told her. "It might take us days, even weeks, to find the right spot. Are you sure you want to start out for there now?"

"Your aunt gave me specific directions. Will that speed things up?"

Taking another deep breath, Michael knew he was doomed. "Probably. So I guess if you're ready, I am, too."

He put the truck in gear and headed out once more. But he wasn't at all positive he was pleased with the way things were going. With Lexie talking to ghosts on a regular basis, no matter what the reason, would she still be the same person as before?

"Uh…while you drive us out of here, do you think I could call Jack?" She reached her hand out for the phone.

Well, he guessed that answered one question.

* * *

Not far from Tocito Wash but on the opposite slope of the Chuska Mountains, two secretive men met behind closed doors.

"The fire wasn't my fault. It was an accident," the one who could turn himself into the Skinwalker Bear whined to his superior. "It got started by a lightning bolt—by the hands of the Blue Flint Boys—perfectly natural. And then I lost sight of the professor's pickup in all the smoke. I had to get myself out, didn't I? But I'll pick up their trail again today."

"I refuse to give those excuses to the Navajo Wolf, you idiot." The Skinwalker first lieutenant, known as the Owl, paced the floor. "The idea behind this scenario of scaring the woman and following her and Michael Ayze around was to make her afraid enough to leave *Dinetah*. The Wolf wants Ayze to find the parchments for us. But that damned do-gooder Brotherhood genius won't be finding anything if he's too busy protecting the woman."

"If you ask me, he's doing more with the woman than just protecting her." The Bear in his human form screwed up his mouth in a ridiculous grin.

The Owl started to wave away the offhand remark then stopped himself, trying to think. There was obviously something between Michael and the Anglo woman. He'd seen the signs himself. Hadn't the Wolf been trying to get rid of the woman for just such a reason?

Could the Owl find a way to use the professor's interest in the woman to the Skinwalker's advantage?

He began to develop a plan. The more he thought of it, the more he decided it would be an ingenious plan.

Turning to the Bear, who was doing his own pacing, the Owl asked, "You're sure you can track them down this morning? And manage to stay with them for a change?"

The Bear shrugged a shoulder. "No problem."

"It'd better not be." The idea budding in his brain was destined to be worth a fortune.

"This time don't let them see you," the Owl demanded. "And I want to know if they seem to be headed toward Monument Valley."

"Do you think they'll go there at long last?"

"Yeah, I do. Finding the parchments before we do is too important to the Brotherhood for Michael Ayze to ignore the search for very long."

The truth was, the Owl knew Michael. Knew him well enough to know what he would do in most situations.

The Owl also prided himself in being an astute observer of human nature. He was positive the woman would behave exactly as he'd imagined in any given circumstance.

"After they leave Monument Valley, I want to know where they're headed from there."

"Probably they'd go back to the Ayze compound, don't you think?"

"Maybe." But if the Owl knew his old friend, they'd be making at least one stop first.

It wouldn't take much to put his new plan into motion. Most of what would be necessary was already set in place.

The Owl smiled and gave himself an imaginary pat on the back. He was a genius. Much smarter than Michael Ayze. Smarter even than the Navajo Wolf.

In fact, after he got his hands on the parchments, he

would turn his attentions back to getting rid of the old Wolf. No rush. Most of his plans for the Navajo Wolf were already in play, as well.

So, yeah. As the teenage recruits would say, he was undoubtedly the smartest—and going to be the richest—badass in all of *Dinetah*.

Lexie blinked her eyes against the harsh sun streaming through the windshield and told Michael which way to turn. They'd been driving for quite a while.

Earlier she'd been overjoyed at finding herself once again on a real asphalt highway and driving past convenience stores and gas stations. But the euphoria had slowly given way to the anticipation of following the ghost's directions and locating the right cave in the desert.

When they'd started out, she'd foolishly hoped their long ride would give Michael and her a chance to talk. She'd even tried a couple of times to introduce the subject.

"Can we talk about last night?" she'd asked boldly when they'd first driven out of Tocito Wash and onto a paved road.

"How far until the next turn?" he asked instead of answering. "You don't need any big distractions right now. We can't have you forgetting the directions. Maybe we can talk about this later."

She had tried talking about it later, too, but met with a similar wall from him.

Michael did manage to do a lot of talking himself, though. He'd absently commented on their surroundings and continued her lessons in the *Dine* Way as they'd traveled through *Dinetah*.

They'd taken the paved road until they reached U.S.

491. Which in turn led them north until they turned on U.S. 64 West. About a half hour later, they made another turn. This time, it was northwest on a graded dirt road at the Tes Nez Iah Trading Post.

From there the directions became less like reading a map and more the way Lexie remembered from living in the back country in Louisiana. *Travel until you pass the double-wide trailer with two medicine hogans in the side yard. Turn left over a cattle guard and go seven more miles until you cross the north fork of Gypsum Creek. When you see an abandoned wagon, turn left again on the rutted sand road and look toward the red rock fingers.*

With every mile they traveled Michael kept up a running lecture on the plants and desert animals they were seeing. She learned to identify chamisa bush, banana yucca and piñon nuts. And heard all about wild deer, desert rabbits and prairie dogs. She even learned more than she'd wanted about the differences between sandstone, shale and granite.

The lessons she'd liked the best, though, had been on Navajo philosophy. Michael talked to her about the Navajo requirement for order and harmony—how every action must have a result. He also compared the Navajo philosophy to Asian philosophy and Confucianism.

He'd told her Navajo beliefs included the idea that thoughts and words can bend individual reality. For instance, to speak of death is to invite it. If you think of joy or sorrow, those are the emotions you will produce.

Lexie was certainly impressed by his knowledge of his heritage. She could see why he was a respected anthropology professor. So brilliant. A wonderful teacher.

While she watched for their next turn, Lexie let

herself lazily gaze out the window, listening to him talk. His words rolled over her skin the way she wished his fingers would. Low and sensual, the tone of his voice both lulled and pulled her.

Just driving. Just talking about plain old rocks. Everything he did was sexy.

At one point in the journey, Lexie even closed her eyes and daydreamed again about last night. The two of them had been so good together. When they'd been in tune physically, it'd felt much as though they were sharing each other's thoughts. Two parts of the same whole.

A part of her was desperate to experience his lovemaking again and again. But another more thoughtful side of her was determined never to give in to that kind of uncontrolled passion again. The pain and loneliness of the day after hadn't quite seemed worth the pleasure.

She steeled herself and tried to behave in the Way of the Navajo, following the lessons he'd given. She cleared her mind of negativity and only thought of the joys and thrills of their lovemaking.

Except for Jack's birth, last night had been the best one of her life.

Once more her thoughts slipped around to this morning's pain of silence, and she felt herself going over to the dark side of anger. His refusal to talk about what had happened, and what might happen in the future between them was just plain killing her.

Did he feel guilty about something? Perhaps he did, but she certainly didn't. And why should he feel guilty? It wasn't like he'd forced her to do anything she hadn't wanted to do. She'd been a full and *very* willing participant.

Damn Michael Ayze and all his tender looks and clever fingers. And damn herself for having given in to him. Lexie swore she would become stronger. She had to be for Jack's sake and for their future here. Last night would be the one and only time letting herself go with Michael Ayze.

"What's next?" His question broke through her thoughts.

"Huh?" She looked over at him and remembered their mission. "Oh, the directions. I think we must be almost there."

"I agree. We've come around a different way than usual, but we're on the outskirts of Mystery Valley where most of the pictographs have been found."

"Let me re-create the directions in my head for a minute." She ran through the various turns in the ghost's directions. "This must be where we get out and walk."

Michael nodded and drove the pickup out of the ruts and onto a hard-packed dirt turnout. "Before you get out," he said as he turned to her. "Let me get you a hat from my pack in the back. The sun can be cruel in the desert."

Crueler than Michael Ayze could be? She doubted it. He'd done everything in his power to make her fall in love with him and then dumped her flat. If that wasn't a perfect definition of cruelty, she didn't...

Love? No. No. No. Absolutely not. She'd sworn she would never be so stupid. It was not possible.

"Take another drink of water, Lexie." Michael held out the canteen and she took it gladly.

They'd been walking in the desert, searching and trying to follow the ghost's directions, for what seemed like hours. But according to her watch, it had only been about forty-five minutes. The midday heat must have fried her brain, making her forget the instructions and lose track of time.

She swallowed sand along with the water, took another gulp and then sat on a flat-topped granite outcropping. "Are we lost?"

He shook his head. "You look flushed though. Our goal shouldn't be more than a few minutes ahead. Are you going to make it?"

Taking another drink, she closed her eyes and thought of Jack. Her baby's future was as a Navajo. She would be the mother of a strong Navajo man.

Grateful for the opportunity to help rid her child's nation of the evil running rampant here, Lexie filled her lungs with air and straightened her shoulders. She renewed her determination to see the job as Message Bearer through to the end.

"I'll be fine," she told Michael. "We're supposed to walk two hundred paces west from the last rock slab of painted images."

"I remember what you've already told me," he said softly. "Another few yards ahead and we should see the cleft where we'll find the cave entrance."

She tried to stand on wobbly legs. Michael took her by the arm, holding her upright until he could slip an arm around her waist to steady her even more.

"Just lean on me, love," he whispered hoarsely. "We'll make it there together."

He was right, too. They hadn't walked far until she spotted the dark patch behind the gray boulders and reddish cliff walls.

"That's it?"

"Yeah, you got us here, Lexie. Just like you were told to do." He showed her how to duck behind a natural overhang and then duck again to enter the cave. "Be proud of yourself. Those directions were complicated, especially for someone unfamiliar with the area."

Lexie didn't feel proud. She wasn't sure what she felt. The minute they'd entered the dark, quiet cave, cold air had brought her temperature and her mind back to normal in a hurry.

Michael took a huge lantern-type flashlight from his backpack. "The petroglyphs must be much farther back in the cave. Otherwise the anthropologists who work this area all the time would've found them long before now. It could be a difficult path. Why don't you sit here near the entrance and wait for me?"

She didn't want him to go alone, but she was exhausted. "How long will you be? Are you sure you won't need me?"

"I don't know how long this will take." He pulled off his heavy-looking backpack and unhooked the long rope he'd attached to it earlier. "You can rest against my backpack. Sit right here where there is still some light filtering in from the cave opening."

"Are you sure you'll be okay?" She lowered the padded case she'd been carrying and handed it over to him. "Can you take your computer with you and still hold the rope and the flashlight?"

"No problem." He put the laptop's strap around his own neck. "Noise echoes in caves. If you need help, just scream. I'm not going so far that I can't get back to you in a hurry if necessary."

"I'll be fine," she told him as she sat.

"Yes, you will." He smiled down at her. "Remember to keep drinking water. Stay hydrated. I'll call out to you every few minutes to let you know what I'm finding."

Lexie gingerly eased into a more comfortable position and watched as he flicked the light out ahead of him into the cave tunnel. Then he disappeared into the darkness.

In a few minutes she heard him call her name. She answered and then relaxed and prepared herself for the wait.

Michael continued to call out from time to time, but his voice got farther and farther away.

Closing her eyes, just for a moment, Lexie tried to stay focused on seeing Jack again so she wouldn't worry so much about Michael.

When she'd talked to her son earlier today, he'd told her all about the wonderful things he'd been doing. Yesterday he'd gone to his cousins' school and his aunt had said he could go to a head-start program there half days if Lexie would agree. Part of his training would be done in the Navajo language. And Jack's best news was that he'd gotten pony currying lessons from his grandfather.

Her heart thumped at the mere thought of how much she missed her baby. Michael had promised they would be back to his sister's in time to tuck Jack into bed. She could hardly wait.

Lexie must've fallen asleep at some point, because the next thing she knew Michael was shaking her awake. "Come on, sleeping beauty. Aren't you ready to go see your son?"

"Michael? Did you find them? Did you find the right petroglyphs?"

He nodded as he helped her stand. "I did. And I entered them into the computer. It's going to take some heavy-duty translating work, but it looks like we've found our answers. We'll be the first to reach the parchments—long before the Skinwalkers."

With renewed energy, Lexie leapt into the air and threw her arms around his neck. "Thank heaven. That must mean the war will be over soon."

"I hope so." He gently pried her arms away and let them drop back to her sides. "There's nothing more important than beating the Skinwalkers."

She must've had a frown on her face at being pushed away, because he quickly turned his back and began reworking his pack in preparation for the return trip.

After a few moments, he spoke over his shoulder. "On second thought, there *is* something more important. It's Jack. All the *Dine* children are the reason we're fighting this war.

"We do battle with the evil for our homes and our clans," he continued. "And for our hearts—our loves."

In his voice she heard a kind of plea for understanding. But she didn't trust her own heart enough to listen.

Chapter 13

Look at that face. Just look at that magnificent face.

Michael's heart tripped wildly as Lexie smiled over at him from the passenger seat. He'd been sitting like a big lump, driving them out of Monument Valley. He had assumed the most important things were getting her back to civilization and out of his truck as fast as possible.

Now he suddenly felt like someone had just slammed their fist into his chest and told him he needed to slow down. Barely able to breathe due to what he'd just seen on her face, Michael blinked and slowed the pickup.

Such things weren't possible in the real world.

He chanced another glance. And there it was. He'd been right the first time. One look at her and he'd had a vision of his children, his whole future, staring out at him from those expressive hazel eyes.

Turning away from the tantalizing sight, Michael

wondered if he was truly doomed forever. She didn't want him.

There must be something he could do to change her mind about him. Some way to keep her close. Just long enough to undo the damage he'd done and start talking about their futures.

He wanted to keep her safe. But he also wanted her to need him as much as he needed her. Was that possible now?

A stray thought broke through his consciousness. A weird thought, about his parents' relationship. How had his father managed to find the right answers to win over his own bride? Michael knew his parents' marriage hadn't started out with love. Their marriage had been arranged by their traditional families, yet they always seemed happy enough.

As he drove toward his sister's house, Michael's thoughts continued winding round and round. His mother. An arranged marriage. Could that be a possibility for him, too?

Maybe he needed to have a long talk with his mother. He needed an ally—and soon.

"You're sure you don't mind?" he asked Lexie as he turned the pickup into the college lot. "It'll only take a few minutes to find the reference book I need then we can be on our way."

She shook her head and stared out the window. "With all those books you have in your home library it's hard to believe you need one more, but I don't mind if we stop at the college for a few minutes. It's still light out. Jack will no doubt be more interested in his afternoon pony riding lessons than he will be in seeing his mom."

The melancholy was clear in her voice. He felt his heart prick in sympathy with the loving mother who'd had to leave her own child.

"What's going on here?" she asked as they pulled into the campus parking lot and saw people and cars everywhere.

"Looks like there was a parade of some sort," he said with a shrug. "I'd guess it's just now breaking up. The kids were probably protesting something. That sort of thing seems to happen a lot on *Dine* campuses."

Several small groups of young people were standing around, some of them having animated conversations. Michael found a parking spot a little apart from everyone and cut the engine. He had been prepared to take Lexie with him as he ran into his office, but there were plenty of people milling outside this afternoon. She should be safe enough in the crowd for a few minutes.

"Lock yourself in and roll the windows down just a crack. I'll leave the keys in the ignition in case you want to turn on the air conditioner. I'm going to take my laptop with me so I can match up some of the pictographs with the right reference book. But I won't be long." He opened his door then turned back to her. "You'll be okay, won't you?"

"Of course. Don't worry." She smiled at him again, but the move seemed to take a heroic effort. He could see the deep smudges of exhaustion and worry under her eyes.

He jumped out of the truck and pressed the door locks behind him. Taking off toward his office with his laptop slung over one shoulder, he listened for any signs of Skinwalkers. He heard nothing except for the sounds of students talking and laughing together.

Michael felt reassured. Temporarily at least, everything was normal.

Lexie closed her eyes and leaned her head back against the headrest. It seemed like a thousand years had passed since they'd last been on this campus. Was it only yesterday or the day before?

Her body felt tired. But it was a good tired. The message she'd given Michael had helped him to locate something important to the Brotherhood.

Yawning, she got more comfortable. But it seemed as if she'd only had her eyes closed for a minute or two at most when they popped open again. Something felt wrong.

The sky had suddenly turned that lavender twilight color she'd seen once before in the high desert. And the background noises of the kids and cars she'd barely been aware of had grown silent.

She turned her head to see if everyone had left her all alone in the parking lot. But what she saw sent a chill up her spine. A group of male students had gathered around the pickup, standing in a semicircle about ten feet from her, and they didn't look too friendly. In fact, a few of them seemed downright angry about something.

No one spoke. No one moved. They simply stood out there glaring at her.

Swallowing back a slice of fear, Lexie fought her nerves and tried to decide what to do. Should she roll the window down and talk to them? Getting that close didn't seem very smart.

What did they want with her? If she climbed out of the truck and went in search of Michael, would the crowd turn into a mob and hurt her?

Minutes went by. Long, scary minutes.

Just when Lexie was about to scoot over to the driver's side and start the engine in case she needed to make a quick getaway, she heard a high-pitched woman's voice speaking in Navajo. After a second or two, she spotted a Native American woman pushing through the crowd. Lexie recognized her right away as the assistant professor Michael had introduced. What was the name again?

Lexie remembered her name just as Amber Billie stepped to the side of the pickup and knocked on the driver's window. "These idiots are leaving." She waved at the crowd with deliberate movements until they began dispersing. "But I think I'd better sit with you. To be on the safe side."

Lexie took her first real breath since she'd opened her eyes, then she unlocked the doors. Amber climbed in behind the wheel and locked up after herself.

"Are you okay?"

"I guess so," Lexie replied, noticing her voice sounded shaky. "What was wrong with those people? What did they want?"

Amber shook her head and rolled her eyes. "They were just a few stragglers left from the Save The *Dine* From Witchcraft protest march. A bunch of trouble-makers, that's all."

"But why did they seem so mad at me?"

The corners of Amber's mouth lifted in a wry smile. "For one thing, you've become the subject of some wild rumors around the college over the last few days. And for another thing, having Get Out Witch! painted on the side of the pickup might not be the best idea if you don't want to be bothered."

Lexie had totally forgotten about the paint. She shifted to look out her side window as most of the crowd wandered away—though she heard some of them grumbling under their breaths.

"Thanks for coming to my rescue," she told Amber without turning around. "I'm glad you were here."

"What are you doing just sitting alone in the college parking lot?"

Lexie looked back and saw the concern in Amber's deep chocolate eyes. "Michael came to get a reference book from his office. He said he wouldn't be long."

Amber nodded. "Good. Then where are you headed from here?"

"To Michael's sister's house to see my son. Why?"

"You have a son? A Navajo child?"

"Yes, of course. My deceased husband, Michael's brother Daniel, was his father. What's wrong?"

Amber shifted in her seat. "I realize you don't know much about our traditions." The expression on the pretty assistant professor's face was serious and troubled. "But you must see how things would appear to others. Especially, to those people whose lives are ruled by superstition and fear.

"As far as anyone can tell from a distance," Amber continued, "bad things tend to follow you around. After all, your car was caught in a flash flood. And we've heard a wildfire chased you down the mountainside. Natural catastrophes don't seem coincidental when they're happening one right after the other to the same person."

"But—"

"I wouldn't worry too much about it if I were you, though," Amber cut in reassuringly. "After all, you'll probably be leaving the rez soon anyway. Your witchcraft concerns and other problems will all dry up when you can put this place behind you."

The growing lump in Lexie's throat threatened to choke her. "Actually, I've decided to stay. My son likes it here with his relatives. I want him to learn his father's traditions, learn the language. And he wants to go to school and act like a real Navajo child."

Amber lifted her chin and flipped her long hair off her shoulder. "I hate to tell you this, but your son won't be welcome at any traditional school. If his mother is considered a witch, the other kids will make his life miserable. They won't play with him or make friends. Their parents won't let them get anywhere near him."

Lexie didn't know what to say. This whole witch business seemed as unbelievable to her as the idea of Skinwalkers had at first. But she guessed it wasn't really such a stretch to believe that a stranger would think a woman who talked to ghosts was probably a witch.

"How can I fix things?" she finally asked, letting her eyes plead with Amber for advice. "I can't stand aside and let my child go through that. Is there anything I can do differently to make life better for him here?"

Perhaps, Lexie thought, it might help if she refused to be the delivery person for any more messages. But when she thought the rest of it over, there wasn't much she could change about the natural disasters that seemed to follow her around. She may as well be the Message Bearer.

"If you were *Dine* yourself," Amber began, after she'd screwed her mouth up in thought, "you could have a special Sing done. That would change the way you're perceived as far as the traditionalists are concerned. But—"

"Michael and I have been looking for the old medicine man who can do just that," Lexie interrupted. "When we find him and have the Sing done, won't I be cured?"

Amber patted her hand. "The only way a Sing would help is if the People thought you were truly following the Navajo traditions and believed in them. Otherwise, it would just look like you were playacting for appearances sake and that would make things worse."

"Why couldn't I do it for real then? Follow the traditions, I mean. What else are the requirements?"

"Following the Navajo Way would take an entire life change on your part. I'm not sure you—"

"I'm willing. I've wanted to do that anyway for my son's sake. I've even been getting lessons from Michael. What are the other requirements?"

Amber sat back and seemed to be studying her. "There's one big thing I can think of that would definitely help your cause. But…well—"

"What? I'll do whatever it takes. Tell me, please."

Amber took a deep breath and then smiled. "Okay, but remember it was you who asked.

"You see, the widow or widower of a traditional Navajo is supposed to marry the deceased's sibling, or at least a first cousin if a brother or sister isn't available. In the long history of the People it's been done that way in order to keep the clans pure and the bloodlines going on into the future. Way back in the day, a single mother with a child was asking for terrible trouble if she tried leaving her family to remarry outside. Her child might be shunned—or worse. So a brother-in-law would step in to offer protection and to become a father for her children.

"But I don't suppose you'd consider doing such a thing today," Amber added with a grin. "It's not something familiar to a modern society, not even in *Dinetah*."

A streak of raw panic flooded Lexie's senses. It wasn't as if she'd never contemplated being Michael's wife. The idea had been floating around in the back of her mind ever since his mother first mentioned it.

But Lexie was mentally exhausted at this point. Simply worn thin from trying to be the sturdy and reliable single mother who'd had to face nightmares she'd never even heard of before. This witch trouble was fast becoming the worst of the lot. She just couldn't handle all the problems alone anymore.

Raising her eyebrows at Amber as if to say *no biggie*, she shrugged a shoulder. "Thanks for the advice. That idea sounds just right for me. In fact, I think my mother-in-law is probably already inviting the wedding guests."

The knock on his office door brought Michael's head up from where he'd buried it in the reference book. He hadn't meant to stay in his office so long, but he'd wanted to make sure the book he collected was the one that could do him the most good with his translations.

Getting up from his desk to unlock the door, he gave the clock on the wall a quick glance and was unhappy to see he'd already left Lexie sitting out in the truck for going on twenty minutes. She would have every right to be angry. He'd known how antsy she'd been to see Jack.

He opened the door, fully expecting to see Lexie standing there with a scowl on her face. "I'm sorry. I completely lost track—"

"Professor Ayze, you need to come quickly." The person on the other side of the door wasn't Lexie. Michael recognized him as that young Assistant Professor Gorman, the damned fool who had probably started the rumors about Lexie being a witch. Gory was not someone Michael had been looking forward to seeing today.

Then the tone of the man's words began to sink in. "What's wrong?" Michael asked roughly.

"Your friend, the Anglo woman, she's in big trouble outside. There's a group of students hanging around who're talking about making her leave the campus. They don't want her kind here. I overheard one of them say something about sending a few rocks her way so she'd be sure to get the point and not come back."

Oh, hell. Michael grabbed for his office key and locked the door in two seconds flat. Without wasting another word, he brushed past Gorman and took off toward the parking lot at a dead run.

What had he been thinking? He should've known better than to leave her alone.

By the time he got within sight of the pickup, Michael's heart was pounding and he was trying to decide the fastest way to drive to the hospital from here. If anything happened to Lexie, it would kill him. He wouldn't want to take so much as another breath of air without her.

But when he hit the edge of the parking lot and looked toward the pickup, he realized there wasn't anyone standing nearby. No gangs of angry teens, nor any student hate groups anywhere in sight. The truck looked as quiet as it had when he'd left it there. Gulping in air, he blinked back the wetness that had been blurring his vision and took a good long look at his pickup.

The words Get Out Witch were more visible than ever. He'd forgotten all about them. He must've lost his mind to keep driving around *Dinetah* like that.

Trying to see if Lexie was still inside the cab through the growing twilight, Michael kept moving and was surprised when he spotted both her and Amber Billie sitting in the front seat. He stopped, taking a moment to compose himself.

"Michael," both women said when he wrenched open the driver's door.

Amber moved quickly and pushed at his chest, making him take a step back while she climbed down out of the cab. "You sure took your sweet time," she told him with a frown and a tap of her foot. "Leaving this woman out here alone was not the smartest thing I've ever seen you do."

"Then there really was trouble?" he asked. He'd been all set to go back and punch that worthless Gorman in the mouth for giving him the scare of his life.

"No," Lexie said from the passenger seat.

"Yes," Amber said at the same time.

He decided it would be best to keep his mouth shut and let the two of them sort it out.

Amber shot Lexie a quick glance over her shoulder and started in. "When I first got here, a crowd of young men I didn't recognize had surrounded your truck. I sent them on their way before things got serious. But I hate to think what might've happened if I hadn't come out when I did."

Pointing to the painted words, she scowled up at him. "Whatever were you thinking to drive to the campus with *that* on the side of the truck?"

Right. He'd been asking himself the very same thing. But it didn't seem too important to explain himself to Amber. Lexie was the one he was most concerned about. She was too quiet.

He stepped into the cab and then turned back for a last word with Amber. "Thanks for helping out. I'm sorry you had to get involved, but I really appreciate it. I owe you one. But now I'd better drive Lexie back to my sister's, before I get into more trouble than I already am."

Starting the pickup, he waited for Amber to step away before shutting the door. As he closed it, though, he saw a smile spread across her face and could've sworn she made another comment as he backed out of the parking space.

He couldn't be sure of what he heard over the engine noise, but he'd thought Amber mumbled something like, "You've got more trouble coming than you can imagine."

When he glanced over at Lexie and found her smiling up at him, too, all thoughts of trouble rushed right out of his head. She wasn't hurt and didn't seem too upset with him. He didn't care what else happened. There could never be any other trouble for him as long as she was okay.

* * *

"I need you to speed things up," Michael whispered to his mother when Lexie had gone to get Jack ready for bed.

Michael and his mother were standing alone in his sister's kitchen putting away the last of the dinner dishes. He'd been so glad to get Lexie back before dark, he'd barely had time to think of anything else but making sure she and Jack were reunited and happy.

His mother put down the dish towel and stared up at him with a twinkle in her eyes. "Any *things* in particular you want speeded up, my son?"

"Don't be cute, Mother. I'm talking about the wedding you're planning. Is there any reason we can't hold the ceremony tomorrow or the next day?"

"That might be a little soon, but it could be arranged. Has the bride agreed to this big change?"

"I sort of thought you might talk to her about it for me," he hedged, feeling like a fool. "Tell her how important it is for her and Jack's future in *Dinetah*."

His mother patted his arm and nodded. "Before supper my daughter-in-law asked me what she should wear for the ceremony, but she never mentioned anything about there being a rush. I must say, though, she seemed every bit as eager as you do."

"She what?" Surely he hadn't heard his mother right.

A grin spread across his mother's face. "Perhaps the two of you need to have a discussion about timing before I start contacting the relatives."

Michael muttered a few choice words under his breath and went off to find his bride-to-be. He found her sitting at the side of her son's bed. The two of them were talking softly as Lexie smoothed the sheets around her son the way Michael had seen his sister do for her kids.

He stood quietly in the shadows of the room's threshold and waited for her to finish what seemed to be a ritual between mother and child.

"Should I call him *Daddy* after you get married?" Jack was asking his mother.

"We'll see if that's what Michael wants. Would you mind if he does?"

Jack shook his head. "No, my angel daddy said it would be okay for me to call him that."

"Your angel daddy? What are you talking about, honey?"

Belatedly it occurred to Michael that there was one more person to be involved in this upcoming marriage. A four-year-old boy who might not have had time to get used to losing one father would now be faced with having a brand-new one. A man he hardly knew.

Michael held his breath and waited to hear what Jack had to say. A child's words suddenly seemed much more important than anything he and Lexie could ever say to each other.

Chapter 14

"You know, Mommy," Jack said earnestly. "My *angel* daddy. Like the picture in your wallet."

Michael heard Lexie's tone of voice change, becoming just the tiniest bit wary, as she said, "When did you see your angel daddy? Were you dreaming?"

Jack shook his head at his mother. "I wasn't dreaming. He came last night and talked to me. You weren't here to tuck me in. My angel daddy did it for you."

"Uh-huh. Did he look like a real person? Like I do, sitting here now?"

"Oh, no, Mommy. He was a *angel*. Not a *really* person."

Michael realized what Jack was saying and knew Lexie had figured it out, too. Her son had seen the ghost of his father last night. Jack had inherited her...talents.

Michael wasn't sure how he felt about that.

But then he thought of Daniel. Michael's heart ached

at the memory of his dead brother. What would Daniel have said about him marrying Lexie and taking over his place with Jack?

"What did your angel daddy say, sweetie?" Lexie's words echoed his own thoughts and came in a hushed whisper, as if she too dreaded hearing what Daniel's ghost would say.

"He said you and Uncle Michael were getting married, and then Uncle Michael would be my new daddy."

"Did he say he thought it would be a good thing?"

Jack nodded. "Sure, Mommy. My angel daddy said Michael was his big brother and he loved him and always took care of him. Now my new daddy will love me and take care of me, too."

Emotion clawed at Michael's throat as he struggled to keep the sudden tears at bay. Was it true Daniel had known he'd loved him all along? The idea was comforting and yet sad at the same time. Why couldn't the two of them have said those words to each other when they'd mattered most?

"Let me hold you a second, sweetheart." Michael heard the emotion in Lexie's voice as she gathered Jack in her arms. "Maybe your new daddy will tuck you in tomorrow night. Would you like that?"

"Okay. But I'm almost too big for tucking. My cousin Ted says so."

Lexie bent her head and kissed the top of her son's head. "You're not too big for loving. That's what I have to say."

Michael set his jaw and stood rigidly, waiting until Lexie finished with her good-nights. As she reached to turn off the bedside lamp, a faint shadow moved over both her and Jack. Michael blinked once in disbelief and the illusion disappeared. Had it been Daniel's way of saying goodbye?

He shook off the crazy notion. But when Lexie backed out of the darkened room and came toward him, Michael felt sure marrying her was his destiny. Their marriage was right and it was bound to be a good thing. For everyone.

Lexie leaned so she could hear what Michael was saying. For such a big guy he certainly could speak softly.

It was late and they were standing on the back porch, trying to be quiet enough not to wake anyone. But as she moved in closer, the heat from his body began setting off internal sparks she couldn't afford to have right now.

The more she was near him, the more in love she became. What a good man Michael Ayze was. Her admiration for him had jumped one thousand percent tonight. Just to think, the man had offered marriage when he didn't even love her. But he would do it anyway, just so she and her son might fit in better on the reservation and hopefully avoid more witch trouble.

Other things were still up in the air. The two of them needed to learn to communicate better if they were going to be husband and wife. Maybe they would actually be married the day after tomorrow, but the terms of the marriage were far from decided.

"Tomorrow we can help move my parents back into their home," he told her. "The next day we'll be married in their ceremonial hogan. Then you and Jack can move over to my house. I'll see about having a paddock built and buying him a pony of his own."

Swallowing her nerves, Lexie nodded her agreement to everything he'd said. But there were other concerns. "What about my curing Sing? When will that happen?"

Michael ran his fingers through his hair. "We still have to find the old medicine man. But I have everyone in the Brotherhood on the lookout. He's bound to turn up soon."

"I guess that will have to be good enough." She looked up at her husband-to-be and saw dark clouds flooding his eyes. "You heard Jack talking about Dan's ghost, didn't you?"

"Yeah, I did."

"Are you upset because my son sees ghosts like I do?"

"Not much I can do about it, is there?"

That wasn't the answer she'd hoped to hear. But it could've been worse. At least Michael had agreed to marry her and become Jack's stepfather, even knowing about the ghosts. Her son was going to get his chance to be a true Navajo.

"We'll have to go to the Navajo Tribal administrative offices at Window Rock tomorrow and take out a marriage license," Michael continued as if the subject of ghosts had not come up. "Everything needs to be done legally."

Lexie couldn't hold back the deep sigh so she looked down at the ground and hid her eyes. "Okay."

Michael put his finger under her chin and lifted her face. "Are you unhappy about something? Would you prefer having a big, splashy Anglo ceremony more like the one you and Daniel had?"

She twisted her face and refused to look at him. "Not at all."

"Then what is it?"

"You haven't once asked me about Dan." Shoot. She hadn't meant to say anything, but now it was out she might as well continue. "At first I convinced myself I loved him. But I grew to know better. What I felt for Dan wasn't real love. I had a big crush on him in the beginning, but the marriage never would've lasted. Dan was a gambler and I know he cheated on me. Before Jack arrived both of us had already been thinking about divorce."

"Our marriage will never end up in divorce, Lexie, if that's what you're afraid of." Michael's voice was rough and his face was half hidden in the shadows. "When you and I marry, it will be for a lifetime."

"Oh, I didn't mean to imply—"

"It's okay," he said, softening his tone. "I know you don't love me. That's no secret. And I know this marriage is mostly for Jack's benefit. But it will still be a commitment for our lifetimes. I won't ever betray you, and I expect you to treat me with the same respect. If that bothers you, or if you can't make promises like those, then back out now."

He didn't know. Was it possible he hadn't been able to read the truth in her eyes? Could she have been so good at pretending she wasn't in love with him that he really believed it?

Unfortunately, Lexie was all too painfully aware she hadn't managed to convince herself. She loved Michael enough to change her whole life for him.

"I'm not backing out," was all she could say.

"Fine." He took a deep breath. "Then I think we'd better get some sleep. There's going to be a lot to accomplish over the next couple of days."

He bent his head to kiss her and she panicked. Pulling back, Lexie silently bit her tongue and shook her head. If he kissed her, she would surely fall into a mangled heap at his feet, and become a quivering mass of desperate jelly. She'd be on her knees begging him to love her in an instant.

Her whole body ached with wanting him. It was terrible to be so totally in love with someone, when that person obviously didn't share the same feelings. After the two of them were married she wouldn't have any choice but to give him the upper hand in their relationship. But until then, she could at least keep her dignity.

Michael frowned down at her through the moonlight. "Our marriage is going to be for real, Alexis. In every way. Don't think otherwise."

He stepped back and studied her face. "But I won't push you for tonight. I know the idea of this arranged marriage may be confusing for you. Once we're married, though, you won't pull away from me. That's part of the commitment."

When she didn't argue with him, he spun around without another word and strode into the house. Which left her puddling in an emotional heap anyway. She might as well have taken the pleasure in letting him kiss her.

"Stolen? You're joking. That can't be." Lexie's face turned ashen and Michael took her elbow to steady her.

Not quite twenty-four hours had passed since they'd become engaged. And not quite fifteen hours remained until they would be married. Michael's thoughts were scattering in ten different directions at once. Lexie was everything he'd dreamed of and all he had been able to think about for days now.

Still, it was hard for him to believe yesterday he'd been so wrapped up in saving Lexie at the college, and then in getting her to marry him, that he'd forgotten about the laptop back at his office. With just a single half hour to spare today, he'd gone dashing back to pick it up. Only to discover the computer had disappeared.

He hated having to admit, after all the hard work and sacrifice in finding those pictographs, their prize was likely now in the hands of the enemy. He felt like a complete fool.

"Afraid it's no joke," he said soberly.

"But who could've stolen it from your office?"

"Excellent question. The Brotherhood will be meeting later to discuss the possibilities. This afternoon my cousin Hunter even went to the cave where you and I located the pictographs, hoping to copy them down again. But they had already been destroyed."

The Brotherhood had lost the momentum in their war, all due to Michael's actions. The *Dine* would pay dearly for his lapse, perhaps forever.

"I hate leaving you on the night before our wedding," he told Lexie. "But this problem is all my fault. I need to find some way to make amends."

She reached over and lightly touched his arm in sympathy. "It's not *all* your fault. Most of the fault is mine, in fact. You weren't the one to start the crazy witch business.

"Please do whatever you need to do." She took a breath and gazed up at him, sincerity shining from those gorgeous eyes. "You're the smartest person I've ever met. If anyone can figure out how to fix things and get the computer back, it'll be you."

Michael fisted his hands to keep from enfolding her in his arms. But it didn't help. As he stood there, lost in the heaven of her gaze, his mind began shutting down again.

Important things became much less so in the waning hours of a dusky day and as he stood transfixed and stared into her eyes. He was struck dumb with the absolute necessity of kissing her. His whole world suddenly came down to just one touch of his lips to hers. It was as if the Skinwalkers did not exist.

"I…" He grazed his knuckles along her jawline. "I lost my balance somewhere out there in the desert the other day, Lexie. But once we're married, I know I'll regain it. You'll guide me through."

He leaned in, desperate to taste. As caught up in her as he was, nothing else mattered but the moment and the passion he was seeing in her eyes.

When he got close enough, though, he saw the same speck of hesitation as he had last night. And now, he watched as her golden hazel eyes clouded with uncertainty. About him?

He cleared his throat and took a step back. "Tell Jack I'll tuck him in another night. I'm sorry, but I have to go. Have my mother explain what will happen during the wedding. I'll see you in the morning."

Not able to stand where he was for even another second, he walked off. He couldn't stay, not when every atom in his body cried out for her. And not when she was looking at him as though he were a gigantic piece of chocolate cake and she had just begun a strict diet.

The next time they were alone they would be

husband and wife. And then, he wouldn't mind at all being dessert. But for now, for one last time, he needed to get the hell away from her before he ruined everything.

Lexie tiptoed out the back door of her in-laws' house and sat on the stoop. It felt a bit frosty outside at this predawn hour, but Lexie had wrapped a heavy jacket around her pajamas. The early morning quarter moon was still illuminating the entire area and a canopy of twinkling stars swirling above her head added their own special brilliance.

Staring up at celestial bodies outlined against an indigo sky brought to mind Michael saying how much he loved clear nights such as this one. She wondered if he was looking up at the same sky from wherever he was tonight. Worry over Michael and all that he faced had been keeping her from sleep.

Wishing she could be by his side to help out, Lexie pulled her knees up under her chin and rested her head in her hands. Her mind went over and over everything, and her thoughts kept turning to the Brotherhood's desperate fight to save the *Dine* from Skinwalkers.

Why did everything seem so mixed-up? Her job as Message Bearer hadn't turned out to be very much help since the computer and the petroglyphs had been stolen. It was even entirely possible her presence had been what cost them the answers. Michael was blaming himself, but Lexie knew he hadn't been the real problem.

What other potential disasters might she end up causing Michael and the Brotherhood?

Later today the two of them were supposed to marry.

But was that really a smart idea? After all, a decent, honorable guy who didn't love her was willing to devote the rest of his life to making her and her son legitimate in the eyes of traditional Navajo. It was exactly what she'd needed and hoped for. But would it mean tragedy for him in the end?

Could she really be so selfish as to ask him to give up his whole future for her?

"You are prepared to accept a message now, daughter-in-law of the Big Medicine Clan?"

As she turned to see who had spoken, Lexie's heart was pounding in double time. There by the door stood the same middle-aged Navajo man's ghost who'd frightened her the first night she'd been in *Dinetah*. But on that night the spirit hadn't spoken, and had only stared and grabbed for her hand.

On the first occasion his ghostly image had woven in and out, right in front of her eyes. Back then the vision of him had blurred together with the image of a wild dog. This time, the sight of the spirit seemed to be more stable—and a lot less scary.

"What do you want with me?" she asked and surprised herself with the strength in her voice.

"You are now ready to carry my message to the Brotherhood. I have been waiting. This is my one chance for salvation and you cannot fail me."

"Excuse me? I don't think I'm ready for anything at the moment. You must be mistaken."

The ghost glared at her, and she decided maybe this spooky spirit was still a *little* frightening.

When he spoke, cold chills having nothing to do with the weather ran down her arms. "I was one of the evil ones during my time in your world, woman. I didn't follow the prescribed Way. And when my life was cut short, I was taken without finding harmony.

"But I have been given one last chance to change the outcome. Do not spurn me, Message Bearer."

"You were a Skinwalker in this life?" Yikes.

"I have been standing by, waiting for you to learn the Way," the ghost told her. "Now you have learned to understand my words, and you will provide access to the Brotherhood."

"Uh…" Lexie wanted to run, but her legs seemed glued to the stoop. Getting away probably wouldn't save her anyway. The ghost would find her no matter where she went.

"You must tell the Brotherhood that *Sarge's* spirit has stayed behind in their world in order to betray the *evil ones*. He has sought out a courier in you, hoping to earn the harmony he seeks in the fourth world. He brings word of an end to the scourge of the Navajo Wolf."

"Well, I suppose I—"

The ghost grabbed her by the arm and it felt like she'd stuck her hand into an ice machine. "You must. I'll give you the directions. You will listen and take the message."

Lexie tugged her arm out of his grip and glared back at the ghost. "Take it easy, will you. What kind of directions?" She was scared but not cowed.

"There is a map buried in *Dinetah*. One showing the way to ancient writings. Writings destined to be the *Dine's* salvation. I have knowledge of where such a map exists."

A map? Lexie remembered Michael talking about a lost map. If this spirit knew the way to find it…

"I'm not sure I believe you," Lexie hedged, not

positive how much she could trust in a former Skin-walker. "But I guess that's not my call. I'll take your message. The Brotherhood will decide what to do."

Just then, the moon dropped behind a cloud, spreading shadows across the entire eerie scene. But as the Skinwalker's ghost began to relay directions for locating the map, Lexie could've sworn she saw a smile gleaming from his dark, haunting eyes.

Michael picked up Lexie's limp hand and noticed how cold her skin still seemed to the touch. The two of them were sitting together in his parents' religious hogan along with Lucas Tso.

A few minutes ago Michael had draped a half-dozen blankets around her shoulders, trying to raise her body temperature. But he could see her continuing to shake and knew her lips were still carrying a slight tinge of blue even after he'd made her drink hot coffee.

She'd called him an hour ago, right before dawn, and tried to explain about another spirit having given her a message. Michael had come home right away, after asking Lucas to accompany him back here to speak with her.

Lucas Tso was the Brotherhood cousin most familiar with hearing and seeing things not of their world. An artist when not working for the Brotherhood, Lucas was known as the *sensitive one*. Finding his dream woman a few months ago had caused him to lose some of his power to hear others' thoughts. But Lucas could still listen with his heart instead of his mind and hear what others often missed. This morning, Michael wanted Lucas's help listening to and deciphering Lexie's ghost story.

"You say this spirit called himself Sarge?" Lucas sat on the other side of Lexie and spoke quietly.

She nodded. "Yeah. He was talking like there was some third person. But I'm sure that's what he meant."

"There was such a man who lived in *Dinetah* and who betrayed his clans as a Skinwalker," Lucas informed her. "Our cousin, Hunter Long, and his new wife were forced to take his life. He died before he could give anyone instructions for finding where he'd hidden a map stolen from the Navajo Wolf."

"His spirit ghost gave *me* those instructions," Lexie said with a raspy voice. "I have them memorized if you will finish writing them down."

Michael was having trouble with the concept, not the directions. He leaned in to look past Lexie and to speak to his cousin.

"Why would a Skinwalker, even the *ghost* of a Skinwalker, want to betray his brothers?" he asked Lucas.

Lexie turned from facing Lucas and stared at Michael with a pained expression. "Is it the ghost you don't believe, or is it me?"

He still had hold of her hand and managed to give it a squeeze before she ripped it from his grip. "I believe you *think* you know what you saw. But it's hard to imagine—"

"Fortunately," she interrupted with a shake of her head, "Lucas seems more inclined to give me the benefit of the doubt."

Michael didn't know what to say, or how to make her understand. She was his whole world. But his world had never included ghosts and spirits of dead Skinwalkers before.

Catching everyone's attention, Lucas reached into his backpack and withdrew a drawing pad and pencil. "Are you willing to try an experiment?" he asked Lexie.

She shrugged. "I guess."

"Good. Then I want you to describe the man you saw."

"The *ghost?*"

Lucas smiled at her. "Yes, the *ghost.* I'll try to draw what you're describing."

Lexie shot him a quizzical look, then nodded and began giving a physical description of what she'd seen. After about ten minutes of Lucas sketching the attributes as she gave them, a picture of a man began to form.

It was a man Michael knew well when he'd been alive. Lucas had drawn the perfect likeness of Levi "Sarge" George, who had been the Executive Director of the Navajo Department of Public Safety before he'd given himself over to witchcraft.

Michael was stunned. He himself had stood over the dead body of Sarge George out in the desert and verified his identity as the dead Skinwalker who'd been able to turn into a wild dog.

"Yes, you've got it right," Lexie said when Lucas was done drawing. "That's the ghost I saw."

Lexie turned back to Michael. "Now do you believe me?"

"It isn't that I don't—"

"Yes, it is. You thought I was dreaming—or lying."

Both of them got to their feet while Lucas turned to a clean page on his pad. Michael dragged her into a far corner and lowered his voice.

"I never once thought you were lying."

"Just dreaming then?" She twisted out of his reach. "I think we'd better put off our wedding. You wouldn't want to be saddled with a wife whose daydreams tend to be realized in terrible ways."

He breathed in. "We *are* going to put off the wedding."

The gasp that came from her mouth cut him clear to the gut. As she narrowed her eyes and lifted her chin, he could see her trying desperately to pretend it didn't matter.

"But only for a few hours," he amended quickly. "Just enough time for the Brotherhood to locate the map."

Her eyes wide, she opened her mouth but no sounds came out. He hoped she would eventually forgive him for giving her the wrong impression. But she'd been so quick to call things off, and he'd wanted to make her think it over.

"I'll go notify everyone of the changes while you and Lucas draw up the directions to the map you have memorized."

They all needed to work fast this time. Fast and smart.

Chapter 15

Lexie paced the floor of her in-laws' medicine hogan, worrying about Michael and trying to find harmony. The family had moved back into their home at the same time as Lucas had finished writing down Sarge's directions to the buried map. Michael had gone to join other members of the Brotherhood to find that map about fifteen minutes ago.

"Would you like me to do a short version of the Blessing Way ceremony for you?" Lucas asked. "It wouldn't take much time and it might bring you peace."

Lexie shook her head quietly. "I'm hoping the old medicine man we've been looking for will be found soon. He'll give me the Sing that I need. But thanks."

She studied Lucas for a moment. "Why didn't you leave with Michael?"

"I thought you might need me."

That was an odd thing to say. But Michael had told her Lucas sometimes said and did strange things. The guy was so soft-spoken and seemed so full of empathy, though, that Lexie felt right at home with this Brotherhood cousin.

Joining him again and sitting cross-legged on the floor, Lexie tilted her head to watch his expression. "You did a terrific job of drawing that portrait of the ghost from what I described. How'd you learn to do that?"

"I've never done that kind of thing before. But as you spoke, I saw a face. Clear and sharp. As if it were a photograph in my hand."

"That's really cool. Do you think you could do the same kind of thing again?"

"Perhaps. Whose face did you have in mind?"

Lexie had been mulling this over for days. Always in the back of her mind, no matter where she went, the image of the Skinwalker Bear as he'd changed into a man kept coming into her consciousness.

"I only saw this man's face for a few seconds. And I was so scared I didn't think I would remember any of it. But I believe I do now. Enough at least to give you a decent description."

"Tell me the circumstances."

"It was early in the morning and I saw a huge bear. I thought it was going to attack Michael so I chased after it throwing rocks."

"You threw rocks at a bear?"

"Well, yeah. But it turned out the thing was a Skinwalker using his animal form. Michael had come running up saying a chant, and then the bear's image sort of melted into a man. I managed a quick glimpse of him from where I was standing, but Michael couldn't see his face at all."

Lucas studied her a moment. "A Skinwalker Bear? Hmm. How big was the man after he'd changed over? Tall or short? Heavyset or thin?"

"Um. He was a big guy. Taller than Michael even. And much, *much* heavier."

"Are you saying fat?"

Lexie nodded and began describing the man she had seen. She surprised herself with how well she could bring the man's face into her mind. And Lucas surprised her even more by drawing him exactly the way she remembered.

When the portrait was almost done, Lucas stopped drawing and stared down at the face he'd drawn. "I've seen this guy before. He works at the college. The name's Gorman, I think."

"I heard Michael talking about a professor there named Gorman," she told him. "I think he might be the one who started the rumors about me being a witch."

Lucas stood up and reached out to help her to her feet, as well. "I'll call Michael and the Brotherhood. We need to locate Gorman right away. Before the other Skinwalkers can spirit him off the way they've done in the past."

Lucas started to leave, but stopped midstride and turned back. "Listen to me, Lexie. I have something to say that has nothing to do with Skinwalkers, but may be just as important to your future.

"I recently married a woman I'd secretly loved for most of my life. It took me much too long to admit my love, though. And I almost lost her because of my silence.

"Don't let the same thing happen to you." Lucas put a hand on her shoulder. "Your *mind* has been telling you to trust in your husband-to-be. But your *heart* hasn't been ready to give him a chance."

"I trust Michael." Lexie wasn't sure she wanted this kind of impromptu lecture from Michael's cousin.

"Not here where it counts the most, you don't," Lucas told her quietly as he fisted a hand against his chest. "Stop thinking so much and let your heart guide the way. It's where the answers lie. You'll find the harmony you seek if you'll just listen to it."

Michael stepped from Hunter Long's SUV following behind Hunter's brother, Kody. He led his two cousins across a skimpy lawn toward Leonard Gorman's ranch-style house. Since they'd spoken to Lucas Tso, the three Brotherhood members had made their way here to confront the suspected Skinwalker. But Michael was still having trouble accepting that Professor Gorman was in fact a real Skinwalker. As a solution to a mystery, it seemed too easy. After all, Gorman had the best access to Michael's office and could have stolen the laptop with ease.

Too obvious. The fool might as well have worn a T-shirt announcing his allegiance to the Navajo Wolf.

Michael, Hunter and FBI agent Kody had driven out here to Gorman's house in order to question the man. If the professor really turned out to be a Skinwalker, Michael knew things would turn dangerous at any moment. That's why all three of them were armed and ready for anything.

Kody knocked on the door and announced himself as an FBI agent. The three men stepped to the sides of the door frame, out of the direct line of fire, and waited for some kind of response from within.

Michael heard rustling noises, coming from the other side of the curtained front window. "Someone's home," he told the others. "And Gorman is known to live alone. So it's probably him in there."

Kody knocked louder. "Open up, Gorman. We want to talk."

Suddenly, a high-pitched buzzing noise split the air. The three Brotherhood men looked up, recognizing the Skinwalker attack alert. Each drew his weapon as Kody made a move to try the doorknob. Michael's whole body vibrated with uneasy feelings.

He reached out and stopped Kody. "Hold it. I don't like this. Breaking down the door now doesn't seem all that smart to me. Let's go check the back and sides of the house before we do anything stupid."

Spinning around, Michael took off, and Hunter and Kody followed along. The three men hadn't gone thirty feet, though, when their entire world exploded in a blast from behind. The noise was deafening. A crush of hot air and splintered wood threw all of them to the ground. The windows and doors had been blown out.

Michael recovered first and made sure both his cousins were okay. Kody had a gash on his forehead from flying glass and Hunter seemed dazed. Michael got them to their feet and pulled each one closer to the road and Hunter's SUV. Just then, another explosion rocked the house. The blast shot fire out the windows and flames licked upward through a hole in the roof.

But this time they were all a safe distance away. Michael called the Navajo Nation Fire Department, then tended to his cousin's wounds with a first aid kit from Hunter's SUV. He thought momentarily about turning around and making his way inside the still burning house to look for the assistant professor. But he was sure it would be a lost cause. He knew Assistant Professor Leonard Gorman would eventually be found dead inside the burned-out shell of his house. It wasn't the first time the Skinwalkers had killed one of their own rather than let him be captured alive.

The Brotherhood was closer than ever to getting their ultimate answers. The map was already in their hands, and they would have the parchments located within days. All thanks to Lexie.

As he thought of her, Michael looked at his watch, checking how much time he had left until their wedding. He needed to change clothes and drive the thirty minutes to his parent's house, all in slightly less than an hour.

Another sharp call sounded from on high then, capturing his attention again. Looking up, he spotted an owl as it soared on the downdrafts. Out of place in broad daylight, the bird was sailing higher on the breezes and flying in large circles, moving in and out of the billowing smoke still coming from the smoldering house.

And of all the weird things, Michael could've sworn he heard that damned owl laughing.

Lexie straightened the folds of the long Navajo skirt around her body and sat down on a lawn chair placed in the position of honor beside a newly lit bonfire. It had been set behind Michael's parents' house. The flames roared and danced. But she'd been paying only half attention to both it and to the sounds of Jack as he played ball with his cousins. Her other half had been listening for Michael's truck to arrive out front.

Her husband-to-be had called a while ago to say the firemen had found Professor Gorman's body. It seemed to her like a horrible way to die. But Michael said Skinwalkers tended to die the way they'd lived. With violence surrounding their hearts and bodies, and evil deeds keeping them from finding harmony.

She'd been sitting here for fifteen minutes, trying to stem a growing case of the jitters—*not* brought on by Michael's near death in the explosion, but more caused by her coming marriage to a man who didn't love her. Soon enough, Michael would show up and she'd be faced with watching him go through with his self-imposed life sentence of a sham marriage.

His family seemed as determined as he was to have the two of them marry. The clans had gathered. The food was prepared. A temporary arbor structure had been built for the ceremony. Everything was ready and they only awaited Michael's arrival to begin.

So Lexie tried to focus on what was going on around her rather than on what the man she loved was preparing to do with his future. She spotted Michael's mother, looking vibrant in an evergreen long-sleeved blouse and matching long skirt with the most beautiful turquoise and silver squash blossom necklace around her neck. The older woman was in her element as she made sure guests were comfortable while they awaited the beginning of the ceremony.

Thrilled by the idea of keeping this intelligent and strong woman in her corner for good, Lexie hoped the life she was preparing to undertake with Michael would turn out to be worthy of her mother-in-law's respect. Michael's father stepped to his wife's side then, and Lexie watched as he whispered something in her ear. Councilman Ayze was dressed in a well-tailored, expensively cut suit. His black hair, streaked with silver, had been combed back off his high forehead. The picture he presented today was both handsome and vital.

The two of them made a grand looking couple. Michael's mother handed her husband a cup of coffee as he smiled and patted her shoulder. They seemed quietly attentive to each other's needs, and the long-lasting bond of admiration and respect between them was obvious to anyone watching.

Maybe, Lexie thought, she and Michael could at least have that same kind of relationship built on mutual respect. She would do anything to make her husband-to-be happy in his life with her. Anything, so Michael never regretted their marriage.

When she heard his truck in the drive, she jumped out of the chair as it toppled over behind her. Lucas Tso and his wife had been standing nearby, and he righted the chair.

"A case of premarriage nerves?" he asked with a sly grin.

"No, not at all," she lied. "I just want the ceremony to begin soon so everyone won't have to keep waiting."

Michael stepped outside from his parents' kitchen door. Lexie watched while he stood, looking over the whole area. When his gaze finally landed on her, she saw his eyes turn dark and stormy. He started out in her direction with a purposeful stride.

Her whole body jerked to attention as he walked toward her. She folded her hands in front to hide the sudden shakes, because she couldn't tell what he was thinking. Had he decided to call the wedding off? Had his brush with death reminded him that life could be too short to waste time tied to someone you didn't love?

She swallowed hard and waited. He stopped just short of her, turning to make a comment to Teal, Lucas's new wife, who was standing with her husband.

Lexie's heart was pounding so loud she couldn't even understand the words the two cousins exchanged. At last, Michael turned around to face her again.

His steamy chocolate eyes gave her no hint as to his mood. "May I speak to you for a moment?"

Uh-oh. This was it. He was going to tell her the wedding was off.

"Sure." Her knees wobbled, but she managed to force a smile aimed toward Lucas and Teal. "Would you excuse us?"

Michael took her elbow and guided her into the house without waiting for his cousin's answer. He stormed the two of them through the kitchen, where several old women stood at the stove preparing fry bread. Then he led her toward the relative quiet of the living room, but veered off at the last moment and rushed them toward the hallway leading to the bedrooms.

Her heart sank. It must be really terrible news if he needed such extreme privacy just to say the words. Silently, deliberately, he walked them down the long hall to a guest bedroom. Ushering her inside the bathroom, he closed and locked the door behind them.

The small space meant the two of them had to stand close together. Too close. Michael's strong, sexy body was taking up most of the room. It was hard for her to catch her breath.

So she took a deep lung full of air and looked up at him. "Michael, you don't need to—"

"Yes, I do," he said in a raw voice as he pushed her back against the wall and clamped his lips on hers in a wild kiss.

Stunned, Lexie clung to him. Hearing herself making odd strangled noises, she felt embarrassed when the sounds came out somewhere between a laugh and a moan. But Michael groaned in response to them, and grazed his teeth along her bottom lip—nipping, tasting and driving her to make still higher sounding notes.

Fast. Violent. Arousing. Devouring her with kisses, he rocked against her body until she could only wrap her arms around his neck and hang on.

As he ran his hands down her sides, he brought more heat and tension curling in her chest. When his hands reached her hips, he cupped her bottom and held her tight. Tight enough to pull her off her feet as he pressed her stomach against the fierceness of his arousal.

With his breath catching and seemingly as labored as hers was, Michael pulled back just enough to gaze into her eyes. The look he gave her was heady, blazing with passion and unmistakable.

"I've been thinking about this for days," he said as he inched her skirt up and ran his hands underneath. "I'm sorry but I can't...I can't wait."

Trying to gulp in air, Lexie was so taken with desire she could barely even think. "But the wedding…the guests."

"They'll wait."

He bunched the skirt around her waist and slid her underpants down. As he palmed her, she began to squirm. He kept gazing into her eyes. His eyes seemed to be begging her to stay with him. It became the most intimate moment she'd ever had, and she nearly passed out from the heat of her own lust.

In the next second, he turned them both in one smooth move, leaning her bottom against the counter. Then he knelt down while he slipped her panties free. Naked below the waist and open to his view, she felt herself getting dizzy as he trailed his hands back up the inside of her thighs and nudged them to open wider. Before she could even catch her breath, he pressed his face to the place that was pulsating and already wet with need. Her whole body jerked a foot in the air when he finally plunged his tongue deep inside her waiting core.

She bit down on her own tongue to keep from screaming out his name. What would his family think of them if they heard her shouts? But the sensations he was creating inside her were just too intense for her to keep still. Whimpering, she squirmed and begged.

"Michael, please," was all she could manage as she drove her fingers through his hair and hung on.

He didn't let up. Soon she felt her whole body shivering and knew she couldn't hold out much longer. Reaching for him, she desperately wanted them to go over together. He only batted her hands away with a chuckle.

"Wait," she mumbled. But in the very next instant, the thickness in her blood sent her beyond waiting. The swift rush of sensation snapping around in her veins brought a riot of pleasure with it. Her head fell back with a moan.

The only thing keeping her in the moment was the knowledge he'd been as crazed with wanting her as she'd been for him. But she couldn't seem to move. Michael stood then and wrapped her tightly in the warmth of his arms.

Still pulsating with her release, she concentrated on reaching for him. But he shook his head and held her immobile.

"You're so beautiful," he said and bent to nibble on her neck.

"But that...that wasn't fair," she muttered, still in a lusty fog.

He let her skirt fall back down around her legs. "I think it was fair. I think it was perfect. Just like you are."

Oh, the man was too much. Her chest hurt as it filled with love. She felt drugged by the force of her need.

"I love you so much," she blurted out without being able to stop herself. "I want to make you as happy as you make me."

"Lexie," he said with a touch of surprise in his voice. "You don't mean that."

Still dazed and not quite thinking, she looked up into his eyes. What she saw almost doubled her over. Certainly she found desire in his expression, but something else lurked underneath all that. Something Lexie had thought she would never find in those intelligent but arrogant eyes.

Vulnerability. He was afraid. Afraid she would hurt him by saying the wrong words.

Choked with the intensity of the moment, she couldn't say a thing. Reaching out, she touched his face, hoping he would be able to read what was in her heart. Hoping he would say what she had longed to hear.

But after a few silent seconds, he dragged his gaze from hers and looked embarrassed. By the time he faced her again, the scared expression was gone and the sexy, arrogant male look was back in its place. She'd lost the momentum. Lost the battle.

He bent to pick up her underwear. "Better get dressed. We can't keep everyone waiting much longer."

Where were the words that should've gone with the vulnerability she'd seen? All that was left to see now was a tightly clenched jaw. She'd taken a big risk by handing him her heart. And she gotten exactly what she should've expected in return. Great sex seemed to be the only thing they had going between them. But well, she guessed it could be worse. Good marriages had been made on a lot less.

When he tried to hand her panties over, she refused to take them. "Keep them in your pocket for me, will you? They'll be a great reminder of what you still have to look forward to after we're married."

Michael groaned. "You expect me to get through the ceremony knowing you're naked underneath that skirt?"

"Yep." She straightened, tucked in her blouse and fluffed her hair. "That ought to keep you paying attention."

With a smug smile and a soft, self-deprecating laugh, Lexie unlocked the door and walked out. If sex was all they had, she would make the best of it. Theirs was going to be one very interesting marriage.

He should be relieved, Michael told himself as the two of them walked outside and headed toward the marriage arbor. The sex between them was better than spectacular. Lexie had been so incredibly responsive to him. Her body was amazing with all that soft, silky skin. Their marriage would definitely stay hot and exciting for a lifetime.

As she'd cooled down from his touches, though, he'd seen that the expression on her face wasn't quite as happy and content as he'd dreamed it would be. She'd walked out of the bathroom all full of feminine sass. But behind her eyes was a bruised look he couldn't quite get past.

Confused, he tried to put things together. Why the obviously phony words of love? Had she only been trying to get back at him for taking her over the edge alone? If she truly loved him, Lexie would've said so long ago. He didn't know her to be devious, but the battered look in her eyes worried him. If she was mad, he would have to find a way to make things right again. But he wasn't sorry for what he'd done.

He'd been crazed with wanting her from the instant he'd spotted her, waiting outside for him to make their marriage vows. He had needed to feel alive again after seeing death and destruction up close at the Skin-walker's. He'd known she would bring him back to life. He just hadn't thought through the consequences.

Looking over to her now in the sunshine, he saw the way her chin lifted as they walked into the circle of his clan and friends. Traditionally, wedding ceremonies would be done at night and at the bride's parents' home. But their wedding would take place in daylight and in front of his family only. Except for Jack, she had no one.

Most of the ceremony would be in keeping with tradition. The temporary arbor, set up to resemble a hogan, had been constructed to signify the newlyweds starting off as an independent family with their own home and the privacy they needed.

When they approached the arbor, Lexie split off and Michael's mother stepped to his side. The groom was traditionally supposed to take his place at the west side of the hogan with his mother sitting beside him. Michael worried about Lexie not having relatives in attendance, but was somewhat placated knowing his cousins' wives were her attendants.

After he and his family sat down on the hogan floor, the bride appeared and his heart skipped. She was carrying a Navajo wedding basket, made especially for the occasion. It was half-filled with white corn mush, as was the custom. Walking behind her and carrying a water jug, was his cousin Ben, who would conduct the ceremony.

Everything went smoothly. Lexie sat in her place beside him on the south side. Ben, acting as medicine man, poured water over both their hands in a washing ceremony, meant to cleanse body, mind and spirit. Then he blessed the basket of mush by sprinkling corn pollen from all four directions.

It was a solemn moment for Michael, and a lump formed in his throat. He shot a glance toward his bride, wondering if she would understand the symbolism. If the meanings behind the two of them being united by the four corners of the Navajo universe were clear to her.

After the corn blessing, the wedding was supposed to continue outside. With everyone sharing the traditional meal, and with the elders advising the new couple about married life.

As his clan and friends rose to their feet, though, Michael was compelled to say something more to his new bride. Something untraditional.

He held up his hand for quiet, then turned to Lexie and took her hand. "My darling wife," he began. "I know you may not understand the complete significance behind the ceremonial planting of the seeds of our life and love together. But be sure of one thing, my love for you is strong and true. I promise to protect you and your child as my love for you both grows deeper throughout our years together. Never doubt me, or my love."

Lexie's mouth dropped open and tears began filling her eyes as she silently stared up at him. Had he done something wrong? Had his surprise declaration embarrassed her somehow?

"Lexie," he whispered. "Please don't be upset. What did I do?"

"You love me?" she asked on a half sob. Her chin trembled.

"Of course." Confused by the look in her eyes, it took him a full minute until it finally dawned on him what she'd meant. *She hadn't known.* He'd never said the words and she hadn't read his mind.

Totally ignoring the crowd around them, Michael dropped to one knee. "Alexis Ayze," he began formally past the huge lump in his throat. "I love you with everything I have to give and have since the very first day I saw your beautiful face. Your acceptance of our traditions and decision to help our cause only makes me love you more every day. Whatever problems I thought we had mean nothing now. I swear we'll have a good life. I'll make it happen. A life filled with as much love as I can provide, no matter that you don't feel the same way."

She gasped and cupped his face in her hands. "But I love you, too. I already told you that, and I meant every word. Don't you know?"

He looked in her eyes and saw what an idiot he'd been. He could see now that she'd been telling him she loved him, both with and without the words. By just her loving actions. But he'd been blinded by his male pride and hadn't trusted his own heart.

Standing then, he took her in his arms and kissed her with as much feeling as he could put into it. When they came up for air, he held her close for another few seconds, refusing to let her go now that they finally understood each other. She snuggled against him, content and oblivious to the murmurs from their family.

He was content, too. Content and beyond happy now that he'd finally figured out how to say the words of a lifetime. The words that would finally bring them to truth and love.

Epilogue

*H*astiin Dodge Todacheene finished the pollen bless-ing, then began a chant Lexie knew was in praise of the four-sacred mountains. As he sang, she felt the power of his presence, uplifting and spellbinding.

She and Michael had been married for two whole weeks, and one of his cousins had finally located the old medicine man. But he'd agreed only to talk to her.

The two of them sat alone inside the medicine hogan behind Michael's house, her house now, too. She hadn't said anything at all to him yet and wished she could be outside with Michael and Jack in the morning sunshine.

After a few more minutes of chanting, the *hataalii* stopped and spoke to her. "You have been seeing spirits of the dead ones, daughter."

It wasn't a question and she'd been surprised he spoke in English. She didn't dare open her mouth to respond.

"Do you believe you need a curing Sing?" The old man studied her in the low light inside the hogan.

Lexie wasn't so sure she needed this "cure." She had every intention of continuing to see ghosts, for as long as they had messages to give her. Besides, she knew now that her son had inherited the gift. She would have to help him learn to use it, too.

"Yes," the old man said quietly as if she'd spoken the words aloud. "Your son will need your guidance. He is destined for greatness. His spirit will bring the *Dine* into a new age of harmony and peace."

"My Jack?" The question had slipped out.

"Do not question destiny or falter in commitment. You have come far in your journey. But the trek has just begun. Now you have a good warrior walking beside you."

Was this guy saying what she thought? "I don't need a cure?" she guessed. "Not since Michael and I are married."

"There is still evil to conquer. But the dawn is breaking. You must continue to help the Brotherhood on the true path."

A few minutes later, Lexie emerged from the hogan and sought out her husband and son in the bright morning light. She had a duty and purpose in her life, and she didn't need a medicine man cure.

Not since she and Jack had found a whole new world in the arms of the man who loved them.

* * * * *

Keep reading for an exclusive extract from

High-Stakes Honeymoon
by RaeAnne Thayne,

out in July 2008 from
Mills & Boon® Intrigue.

High-Stakes Honeymoon
by RaeAnne Thayne

Olivia sighed, gazing out at the ripple of waves as she tried to drum up a little enthusiasm for the holiday that stretched ahead of her like the vast, undulating surface of the Pacific. She'd been here less than twenty-four hours and had nine more days to go, and at this point she was just about ready to pack up her suitcases and catch the next puddle jumper she could find back to the States.

She was bored and lonely and just plain miserable.

Maybe she should have invited one of her girlfriends to come along for company. Or better yet, she should have just eaten the cost of the plane tickets and stayed back in Fort Worth.

But then she would have had to face the questions and the sympathetic—and not so sympathetic—looks and the resigned disappointment she was entirely too accustomed to seeing in her father's eyes.

No, this way was better. If nothing else, ten days in another country would give her a little time and distance to handle the bitter betrayal of knowing that even in this, Wallace Lambert wouldn't stand behind her. Her father sided with his golden boy, his groomed successor, and couldn't seem to understand why she might possibly object to her fiancé cheating on her with another woman two weeks before their wedding.

It was apparently entirely unreasonable of her to expect a few basic courtesies—minor little things like fidelity and trust—from the man who claimed to adore her and worship the ground she walked on.

Who knew?

The sun slipped further into the water and she

sighed again, angry at herself. So much for her promise that she wouldn't brood about Bradley or her father.

This was her honeymoon and she planned to enjoy herself, damn them both. She could survive nine more days in paradise, in the company of macaws and howler monkeys, iguanas and even a sloth—not to mention her host, whom she had yet to encounter.

James Rafferty, whom she was meeting later for dinner, had built his fortune through online gambling and he had created an exclusive paradise here completely off the grid—no power except through generators, water from wells on the property. Even her cell phone didn't work here.

Nine days without distractions ought to be long enough for her to figure out what she was going to do with the rest of her life. She was twenty-six years old and it was high time she shoved everybody else out of the driver's seat so she could start picking her own direction.

Some kind of animal screamed suddenly, a high, disconcerting sound, and Olivia jumped, suddenly uneasy to realize she was alone down here on the beach.

There were jaguars in this part of the Osa Peninsula, she had read in the guidebook. Jaguars and pumas and who knew what else. A big cat could suddenly spring out of the jungle and drag her into the trees, and no one in the world would ever know what happened to her.

That would certainly be a fitting end to what had to be the world's worst honeymoon.

She shivered and quickly gathered up her things, shaking the sand out of her towel and tossing her sunglasses and paperback into her beach bag along with her cell phone that she couldn't quite sever herself from, despite its uselessness here.

No worries, she told herself. She seemed to remember jaguars hunted at night and it was still a half hour to full dark. Anyway, she had a hard time believing James Rafferty would allow wild predators such as that to roam free on his vast estate.

Still, she wasn't at all sure she could find her way back to her bungalow in the dark, and she needed to shower off the sand and sunscreen and change for dinner.

She had waited too long to return, she quickly discovered. She would have thought the dying rays of the sun would provide enough light for her to make her way back to her bungalow, fifty yards or so from the beach up a moderate incline. But the trail moved through heavy growth, feathery ferns and flowering shrubs and thick trees with vines roped throughout.

What had seemed lovely and exotic on her way down to the beach suddenly seemed darker, almost menacing, in the dusk.

Something rustled in the thick undergrowth to her left. She swallowed a gasp and picked up her pace, those jaguars prowling through her head again.

Next time she would watch the sunset from the comfort of her own little front porch, she decided nervously. Of course, from what the taciturn housekeeper who had brought her food earlier said, this dry sunset was an anomaly this time of year, given the daily rains.

Wasn't it just like Bradley to book their honeymoon destination without any thought that they were arriving in the worst month of the rainy season. She would probably be stuck in her bungalow the entire nine days.

Still grumbling under her breath, she made it only a few more feet before a dark shape suddenly lurched out of the gathering darkness. She uttered a small shriek of surprise and barely managed to keep her footing.

In the fading light, she could only make out a stranger looming over her, dark and menacing. Something long and lethal gleamed silver in the fading light, and a strangled scream escaped her.

He held a machete, a wickedly sharp one, and she gazed at it, riveted like a bug watching a frog's tongue flicking toward it. She couldn't seem to look away as it gleamed in the last fading rays of the sun.

She was going to die alone on her honeymoon in a foreign country in a bikini that showed just how lousy she was at keeping up with her Pilates.

Her only consolation was that the stranger seemed just as surprised to see her. She supposed someone with rape on his mind probably wouldn't waste time staring at her as if she were some kind of freakish sea creature.

Come on. The bikini wasn't *that* bad.

She opened her mouth to say something—she wasn't quite sure what—but before she could come up with anything, he gave a quick look around, then grabbed her from behind, shoving the hand not holding the machete against her mouth.

Right as I'm about to die, I realise all the myths are fake. My life isn't flashing before my eyes. All I can think about is how much I want to live.

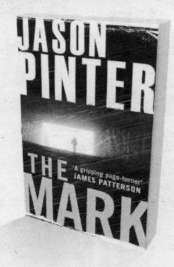

I moved to New York City to become the best journalist the world had seen. And now here I am, twenty-four years old and weary beyond rational thought, a bullet one trigger-pull from ending my life.

I thought I had the story all figured out. I know that both of these men — one an FBI agent, the other an assassin — want me dead, but for very different reasons.

If I die tonight, more people will die tomorrow.

Available 16th May 2008

www.mirabooks.co.uk

FREE!

4 Books
and a surprise gift!

We would like to take this opportunity to thank you for reading this Mills & Boon® book by offering you the chance to take FOUR more specially selected titles from the Intrigue series absolutely FREE! We're also making this offer to introduce you to the benefits of the Mills & Boon® Reader Service™—

* ★ FREE home delivery
* ★ FREE gifts and competitions
* ★ FREE monthly Newsletter
* ★ Exclusive Reader Service offers
* ★ Books available before they're in the shops

Accepting these FREE books and gift places you under no obligation to buy, you may cancel at any time, even after receiving your free shipment. Simply complete your details below and return the entire page to the address below. You don't even need a stamp!

YES! Please send me 4 free Intrigue books and a surprise gift. I understand that unless you hear from me, I will receive 6 superb new titles every month for just £3.15 each, postage and packing free. I am under no obligation to purchase any books and may cancel my subscription at any time. The free books and gift will be mine to keep in any case.

I8ZEF

Ms/Mrs/Miss/Mr ....Initials ....
BLOCK CAPITALS PLEASE
Surname ....
Address ....
....
....Postcode ....

Send this whole page to:
UK: FREEPOST CN81, Croydon, CR9 3WZ